FRACTURED

PERFECTLY IMPERFECT SERIES

souls

NEVA ALTAJ

Fractured Souls
License notes

Editing by Susan Stradiotto and Andie, Beyond The Proof
www.susanstradiotto.comv www.beyondtheproof.ca
Proofreading by Yvette Rebello, reditor.com
Manuscript critique by Anka Lesko, www.amlediting.com

Cover design by Deranged Doctor,
www.derangeddoctordesign.com

Author's Note

Dear reader,

Fractured Souls has been my hardest book to write so far. Because of the delicate subject, it's different from the previous books in the series. *Fractured Souls* focuses mainly on the characters, and while there is a Mafia/crime subplot present, it's secondary to the characters' story. Also, if you've read the previous books in the series, you know I love to throw a bit of humor into each story. This book, however, won't have that element. It deals with an extremely heavy subject, and the inclusion of humor would have been distasteful.

Please read the trigger warning on the next page. If you feel like you may find the subject matter disturbing, or it may cause you harm, please skip this story. Don't worry, if you do decide to pass on this one, you won't miss any revelations critical to the rest of the series, and you will be able to return to the Perfectly Imperfect world in the next book. However, if you're still uncertain whether you should read it, please feel free to email me or reach out via TikTok or Instagram message (my contact information is on my website at www.neva-altaj.com/contact) and share your concerns. I'd be happy to give you spoilers so you can decide if you want to read the book or not. Your mental health matters.

I would like to express my gratitude to Ruthie, who did a sensitivity read for Fractured Souls and offered advice for improvement so that Asya's struggles, and her journey, are presented realistically and tactfully.

If you choose to read *Fractured Souls*, I hope with all my heart that you'll like Asya and Pavel's story. It might be a part of a Mafia series, but above all else, it's the story of love, overcoming hurt, the strength of family, and the perseverance of the human spirit.

Trigger Warning

This book contains topics that may be difficult for some readers, such as an on-page sexual assault (including rape, but not between the main characters), post-traumatic stress disorder (PTSD), mention of attempted suicide, mention of sexual slavery, mention of drug use, explicit scenes of violence and torture, and gore. If you are a survivor of sexual and/or physical abuse, parts of this story may trigger memories that can cause stress or sadness.

Our heroine deals with her situation by relying on the strength and support of our hero. While we believe that love can heal, please keep in mind that this story is a work of fiction. I encourage you to seek out help from a support organization and/or a trusted health professional. You do not need to suffer in silence.

CHARACTER NOTES

Asya—pronounced as [ˈaːzja].

Pasha—Russian nickname (short form) for Pavel, used in casual settings.

Pashenka—a variation (affectionate diminutive) of the name Pavel/Pasha, used as a term of endearment by close family members/relations.

Mishka—a Russian term of endearment, meaning little bear or teddy bear.

> *In case you need to refresh your memory on the*
> *Bratva hierarchy and family ties, check out the*
> *"Extras" page on my website.*

PLAYLIST

There are several classical pieces mentioned throughout the book. Here's the list in case you want to check them out.

"Moonlight Sonata" by Ludwig van Beethoven

"Flight of the Bumblebee" by Nikolai Rimsky-Korsakov

"Gymnopédies" by Erik Satie

"In the Hall of the Mountain King" by Edvard Grieg

"The Rain Must Fall" by Yanni

"Für Elise" by Ludwig van Beethoven

"River Flows in You" by Yiruma

FRACTURED

PERFECTLY IMPERFECT SERIES

souls

Prologue

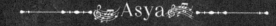 Asya

I T's snowing.

The ground is cold on my back, scraping my shoulder blades, as I stare over the man's shoulder into the dark expanse above me. Everything seems blurry. I can't discern separate snowflakes, but I can feel them falling on my face. Fragile. Delicate. They remind me of the notes in one of the pieces by Erik Satie so I hum the tune while a searing pain keeps tearing at my insides.

Should it hurt this much? I know it was supposed to hurt at first, but I never imagined it would keep hurting.

The man grunts and the weight is suddenly gone. I slide my hand down my stomach and over the fabric of my torn dress to press my palm between my legs. Wetness. Too much. Way too much. I raise my hand in front of my face, staring at my blood-covered fingers while the melody still plays in the back of my mind.

"Well, you've ended up being quite a treat, sweetheart," the male voice says. "I had my eye on your sister initially. You may look the same, but there is just something about her that oozes class. The clients do tend to prefer more polished ones, but you'll do."

Panic, as I've never felt before, explodes in my chest, breaking me out of the stupor I'd fallen into. I roll to the side until I'm lying facedown on the ground. Energy surges through my veins, and I spring to my feet. And then, I run.

The pain between my legs is excruciating. With each step I take, I feel a stabbing jolt. My whole body is shaking, but I'm not sure if it's from the cold, the pain, or the shock. Maybe it's just the horror of what he did and said. I risk a quick look over my shoulder and a low whimper leaves my lips when I see my rapist following and gaining on me.

There are streetlights some distance in front of me, so I change my course to run in that direction. The faint, slow melody playing in my head transforms into a battle march as if urging me to go faster. The ground is uneven, making it hard to run. I keep tripping over the roots of the nearby trees and the small bushes that are hard to see in the dark. My vision is blurry—I lost my glasses—but I focus on the light that I can see through the branches like it's my only lifeline and keep running. The ripping and burning sensations in my lower belly are almost too strong to ignore, but I grit my teeth and try to keep my pace. The air leaves my lungs in short bursts while snowflakes fall on the exposed skin of my arms. Just a few dozen yards to the street. I can hear the vehicles. I just need to reach the street, and someone will stop and help me.

I'm almost there when my bare foot catches on something and I stumble, falling with my face hitting the cold, hard ground. No! I get up, intending to keep running toward the lifesaving light when an arm wraps around my middle from behind.

"Got you!" The son of a bitch laughs.

I scream, but his other hand covers my mouth, stifling the sound.

"It looks like they will have to reeducate you, honey," he says next to my ear. "I might visit you again when you're more docile. Boss lets me fuck my finds for free once a month."

"Please," I whimper into his palm while kicking my legs.

"Perfect." He lets out another wicked laugh. "See, you're already learning."

I try hitting him with my elbow and almost escape his grip when I feel the prick of a needle on the side of my neck.

The man shushes me. "Easy, now. Just a few seconds and it'll all get better."

My vision blurs until there is nothing left but darkness.

The music stops.

CHAPTER
one

Two months later

NEON LIGHTS SHINE DOWN ON PEOPLE CRAMMED together, moving to the music which is blasting from the overhead speakers. The smell of alcohol and competing fragrances permeate the air, even up here, in my office. I step toward the floor-to-ceiling glass wall and cross my arms over my chest, watching the crowd on the dance floor below. It's not even midnight, but it's packed with hardly any breathing space.

A commotion at the far corner of the dance floor attracts my attention. Vladimir, one of the club bouncers, is holding a man by the back of his shirt, dragging him toward the stairs that lead to the upper level. If the man was starting a brawl, security would have thrown him out. This must be something more serious if he is being brought to me.

The door behind me opens five minutes later.

"Mr. Morozov." Vladimir pushes the man inside the office. "We caught this one dealing in front of the restrooms."

I walk toward the man sprawled on the floor and put the sole of my right shoe over his hand. "Distributing drugs in my club?"

The man whimpers and tries to remove my foot with his free hand, but I press harder. "Talk."

"It was just some pills a friend gave me," he chokes out and looks up at me. "He said it's some new stuff he swiped from his work."

I cock my head to the side. "His job? What does he do?"

"I don't know. He never talks about it." He tries to free his hand again but fails. "I'm so sorry. It won't happen again."

I motion for Vladimir to hand me the small plastic bag he's holding and look it over. There are a dozen white pills inside. "Have you tried this?"

"No . . . I . . . I'm not into drugs," the man says, then whimpers when I apply more pressure to his hand.

"So you brought them here to sell. Very wise." I throw the plastic bag back to Vladimir. "Take this to Doc. We need to check what's in that crap."

"What should we do with the dealer?" Vladimir nods toward the man on the floor.

Based on the panicked look in the man's eyes and the shaking of his hand, it wouldn't take long to break him. I could take him to the storeroom and question him. But we have rules in the Chicago Bratva, and my scope of work doesn't include information extraction.

"I think he would enjoy a little chat with Mikhail. Get him out of my sight," I say and turn around to walk back to the glass wall overlooking the dance floor.

I can hear yelling and a lot of kerfuffle behind me as Vladimir drags the man out. The racket ceases when the door closes behind them. My eyes scan the people milling around and dancing, stopping at the booth in the far-left corner. Yuri, the man in charge of the Bratva's soldiers, is sitting in the middle with a blonde-haired woman by his side. On his other side, laughing about something, are the brothers Kostya and Ivan, who manage the finances in our organization. Seems like some of the guys got a free night.

The phone in my pocket rings. I take it out and see Yuri's name on the screen.

"Is something wrong?" I ask when I take the call.

"No," he says, looking up at me from the booth. "Come down and have a drink with us."

"I'm working."

"You're always working, Pasha." He shakes his head.

He's right. Unless I'm sleeping or working out, I'm at one of the Bratva's clubs. Spending time in my empty apartment since I moved out of the Petrov mansion when the pakhan's wife had a child has always been hard. But in the last few years, it's gotten even harder. The fact that I've been running two nightclubs for the last seven years, spending most of my time surrounded by people, should be enough to make me want to seek solitude. It's not. It just reminds me that I have no one to go home to.

"Come on, just one drink," Yuri urges again.

Kostya's deep laugh comes through the line. Looks like he's fooling around again. Always a trickster, that one. "Some other time, Yuri," I say.

I end the call but don't move away from the glass wall, watching my comrades having a great time. Maybe I should join them. It would be nice to relax and talk about nonsense sometimes, but I never can. The problem is, on the few occasions I have gone out with them, I ended up feeling even more alone.

The Bratva is the closest thing to a family I've ever had. I know for sure that each one of them would take a bullet for me. As I would for them. And still, even after ten years in the Bratva, I can't let myself get too close to my friends. With my past, I guess, this may be expected. When you're discarded by the people who should have been your safe harbor, it's hard to allow yourself to get close to anyone because, at some point, they will leave, too.

Sooner or later, everyone leaves.

I stand there for a long time, watching the guys laugh, then turn away and go back to work.

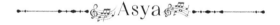

Asya

I walk inside the office and come to a stop in the center of the room. Dolly, the woman in charge of the girls, is sitting behind her desk, her attention focused on the small leather-bound notebook in front of her.

"You'll be entertaining Mr. Miller tonight," she says as she scribes something in her ledger. "He prefers it slow. Start with a massage and go from there."

I nod. "Yes, Dolly."

"Oh, and no blow jobs. Mr. Miller doesn't like those." She closes the notebook and walks around the desk, her heels clicking against the linoleum. I bow my head and focus my gaze on the floor so she won't be able to see my eyes. Her pink shiny heels enter my field of vision as she comes to a stop right in front of me.

"He's a very important client, so make sure you fulfill his every need. If he likes you, he may request you again. He's very mild-mannered. He doesn't hit girls often, which is rare as you already know. And don't forget the condom. You know the rules."

I nod again and raise my hand, palm up. Dolly places a single white pill on my palm.

"What about the rest?" I ask. "I need more. Please."

"Always the same tune with you girls," she barks. "You get the rest when you're finished with the client. You know that already."

"Just one more," I beg.

"I said after you are done!" she yells and slaps me across the cheek. "Get back to your room and be ready in an hour. You've been out of commission for almost a week. We're losing money."

"Yes, Dolly," I say in a small voice and turn toward the door.

"Oh, and don't forget to take off the glasses. Mr. Miller doesn't like those."

"Of course," I say.

After exiting Dolly's office, I turn left and hurry down the hallway, passing the doors to other rooms. I'm one of five girls here at the moment. There used to be six of us, but two days ago, one of the girls disappeared. Since I try to keep to myself, I didn't know her other than seeing her in passing. I remember she had long blonde hair which she wore braided down her back. No one knows what happened, but I heard the other girls gossiping about her meeting with a client who is known to be rough.

I reach the last door at the end of the hallway and walk inside. After a quick look around to make sure my roommate isn't here, I rush toward the small bathroom on the other side of the room. I lock the door and turn toward the toilet.

Opening my right hand, I stare at the white pill in my palm. Such a small thing. Harmless looking. Who would guess that something so tiny can keep a person willfully enslaved, living in a prison without bars? It would be so easy to put it into my mouth and just . . . let go.

It is always the same setup. One pill before the meeting with the client. Three more after I'm done. The first one is meant to keep me high and, therefore, more obedient. It doesn't make it hurt less, but it does make me not care. It's also highly addictive. If I take it, it will ensure I'll come rushing back for the three pills afterward to satisfy the craving brought on by the first. The cycle would repeat. Again, and again. Keeping my brain in a haze, constantly on some level of high, needing more each time, not capable of thinking about anything else.

An addict, that's what I've become. Just like the rest of the girls here.

I squeeze the pill in my hand, then throw it into the bowl and flush it. The pill makes two circles before disappearing down the drain, but I keep standing there, staring into the toilet.

It's been six days since I stopped taking the drugs. It happened by accident. I caught stomach flu last week, and for three days, I vomited nonstop. My body wouldn't keep anything inside, including the pills Dolly continued to shove down my throat. By the time I felt better, my brain was clear of the drug-induced stupor for the first time in two months.

That day was the hardest. Even though I was constantly cold—God, I don't ever remember being so cold in my life—I was sweating. Everything hurt. My head, my legs, my arms. It was like every single bone in my body had been shattered. And then there were the tremors. I tried to control the shaking for fear my teeth would fracture, but couldn't. Dolly thought it was the fever finally breaking, but it wasn't. It was withdrawal. The urge to just swallow the pills she gave me was almost too much to fight, and only pure stubbornness kept me from succumbing.

It got easier after that. I still randomly got the chills, but it was nowhere near what I experienced that first drug-free day, and my limbs and head hurt significantly less. I pretended to swallow the pills and made sure to act the same as I did before, begging for more all the time, while secretly throwing the drugs away. Amazingly, my deception worked. Now it's just a question of how long I'll be able to keep the pretense before someone notices.

I take off my glasses and leave them next to the sink. They aren't even the right prescription, just something Dolly got me so I would stop stumbling and squinting. My own were lost during my last night in New York.

I look away from the reminder, take off my clothes, and step inside the shower stall. Turning the water to scorching hot, I move under the spray and close my eyes. There is a washcloth on the small shelf to my right. I take it and scrub my skin until it's red, but it doesn't help. I still feel filthy.

I don't understand why I haven't fought harder. Yes, the drugs kept my brain in a haze, but I've always been aware of what was happening. Still, I've just . . . capitulated. Let them sell me, night after night, to rich men who are willing to pay an enormous amount of money to fuck a pretty, polished doll. Because that's what we are. They wax us, have our nails and hair done, and make sure we wear expensive clothes. The full face of makeup is mandatory, and it smears quite nicely when a girl cries after the session. So many of the men like to see us break.

I haven't cried once. Maybe something broke inside me that first night. A million particles of my fractured soul mixed with the snow and blood. I just didn't care anymore.

The driver comes to pick me up an hour later, and during the drive, I stare blankly through the window at the people rushing along the unfamiliar sidewalks. When I was taken, at first I thought I was being held somewhere on the outskirts of New York, but I now know that I've ended up in Chicago. As I watch "normal life" passing me by, for the first time in two months, I'm tempted to grab the handle and try to escape. I'm sickened at the realization that it's taken me this long to think about running away. But I consider it now. I want to feel clean again. That may never happen, but I want to try.

I've heard what they do to girls who try to escape. As long as we are obedient, we get the pills, because high-paying clients don't like girls with needle marks on their bodies. But the moment a girl creates problems, they switch to the syringe. And it's over. Was that what happened to the girl who disappeared?

Leaning back in the seat, I close my eyes and exhale. I'll keep pretending I'm still an obedient little slut, ready to endure everything and wait for my opportunity. I will have only one chance, so I better make sure it counts.

They always wear suits.

I regard the man sitting on the edge of the bed in this fancy room where the driver escorted me. Late fifties. Receding hairline. He's wearing an impeccable gray suit and an expensive watch on his wrist. Two phones on the nightstand. Probably a banker. Again.

The room is as expected for a client like him. Heavy luxury curtains in deep red—the color of blood—and a four-poster bed with black silk sheets to hide the bloodstains. A tall lamp in each corner and a wooden mobile bar stocked with different liquors. Only the best labels, of course. I've been in this room once before, but I remember that the bathroom is equally chic, with a large tub and a shower. There's a first aid kit under the sink there. The driver used it because the client I was with that night left me with a nasty cut on my lip.

Mr. Miller motions for me to approach. I close the distance between us and stand between his legs, trying to detach myself from what will follow. It was much easier with the pills.

"Pretty," he says and places his palm on my thigh just below the hem of my short white dress. Seems like it's the favorite color of every client. "How old are you?"

"I'm eighteen, Mr. Miller."

"So young." His hand travels upward, pulling my dress. "Call me Jonny."

"Yes, Jonny," I mutter.

"Dolly said your name is Daisy. Small and sweet. Fitting." A shiver passes over my body upon hearing the name they gave me because they found my own too unusual. I despise it. Just hearing it makes me want to throw up.

Mr. Miller lifts my dress over my head and throws it onto the floor. It falls as a small white bundle at my feet. I don't know why, but clients removing my dress has always hit me harder than them taking off my panties. Each time it happens, it feels like the last layer of my defense is stripped away from me. I shudder.

"Do you find me attractive, little Daisy?" he circles my waist with his hands.

"Of course I do, Jonny," I say automatically. It had been ingrained in my brain with fists during my first day of training.

"Hmm . . ." His hands squeeze my waist, then pull my lacy thong, white as well, down my legs. "I usually like it slow. But you are too sweet. I don't think I can wait."

The moment he has my panties removed, he throws me onto the bed. I lie there, unmoving, and watch him take off his jacket. His tie is next, and my body shakes as he loosens the knot. One of my previous clients wrapped his tie around my neck while he fucked me from behind, pulling on it every time he thrust into me, cutting off my air. I close my eyes in relief when Mr. Miller throws his tie to the floor. He starts on his dress shirt, but only undoes the first two buttons and moves to his pants. My breathing pace picks up. At least he removed the tie. I can handle the shirt.

"Open your legs wide, honeybee," he says as he puts on the condom. The guy who runs the organization is very strict on protection, but it's more about making sure the clients are safe than the girls' safety.

Mr. Miller crawls across the bed until he is looming above me. The vein at the side of his neck pulses. He watches me with wide eyes, then dips his head and licks my naked breast. I grit my teeth together, willing myself not to recoil. It doesn't end well when I recoil. I hope the music will come, making this a little easier to block out. It doesn't. The last time I heard the music was that snowy night. Sometimes, when I lie in bed, trying to sleep, I drum my fingers on the bedside as if it'll help call the melody. But I don't hear it like I used to.

Mr. Miller's meaty hands grip the inside of my thighs, spreading my legs apart. The next moment, his cock thrusts inside me all at once.

It hurts. It always hurts, but without the drugs to scramble my mind, it's a thousand times worse. I tilt my head up and stare at the ceiling as he slams into me again. At times like these, I try to disconnect, to mentally pull away and toward a happy memory, hoping to detach myself from yet another rape.

Thank God, a memory pops into my brain.

It's the summer before my sophomore year of high school. I'm sitting in the garden, reading, while my twin sister chases her Maltese—Bonbon—across the lawn. Poor animal. She even put a yellow silk bow on his head. When Sienna said she wanted a dog, I was sure Arturo would say no. Our brother is not a fan of keeping animals inside the house. I have no idea how she managed to convince him to let her have one.

"Asya!" Sienna yells. "Come!"

I wave my hand at her and keep reading. The murder mystery is just being unraveled, and I'm eager to see who the culprit is. I'm sure it's . . .

A spray of cold water splashes my chest. I scream and jump up off the chair, glaring at my sister. She's holding a watering hose in her hand, laughing like a madwoman.

"You're dead!" I chuckle and dash toward her. She's still doubled over from laughter when I reach her. I grab the hose, pull the collar of her top, and send the water stream down her back.

Sienna shrieks and turns, then grabs the hose, trying to direct it at me, but it just ends up spraying her face. I'm still laughing when I lift my free hand to wipe the water from my eyes, but I stop mid-motion. My hand is red. I look at the hose in my grip. It's pouring red liquid onto the ground around my feet. Blood.

I open my eyes and stare at the white ceiling above me while the smell of sweat infiltrates my nostrils. Yeah . . . the happy memory trick never works that well.

Mr. Miller keeps pounding into me, his labored breaths blowing into my face, and beads of sweat dripping onto me. He groans loudly, the sound reminding me of some huge animal in rage. Abruptly, he stops and pulls out. His weight disappears. I lift my head off the pillow and see him slumped on his knees at the foot of the bed, his hands clawing at his chest. He's breathing hard. His face is red as he stares at me with wide eyes.

"The . . . pills," he chokes out. "In . . . the jacket."

I just gape at him for a few moments before getting up off the bed and running toward his jacket where he had left it on the back of a chair. I find an orange bottle in the left pocket and take it out. Mr. Miller is slumped on all fours, trying to draw breath.

"Give me . . ." he wheezes, raising his arm in my direction.

I look down at the bottle in my hand and back up, taking in his flustered face and rheumy eyes. Slowly, I step further back. Mr. Miller's enormous eyes glare at me. I retreat a few more steps until I feel the wall behind my back.

And then, I watch.

It lasts less than two minutes. Wheezing. Shallow, labored breaths. And finally, a choking sound. Mr. Miller collapses sideways onto the bed, his head tilted up in my direction, eyes bulging. It looks like he is trying to speak, but the words are jumbled. I can't make out what he's saying, but I see it on his face. He is begging. I stay rooted to the spot, clutching the medicine bottle in my hand, and watch a man dying before my eyes. With each breath he takes, I feel the remains of my soul, or whatever is left inside me, die a little more. Until there is nothing, just a black hole.

The door on my left bangs open and my driver barges inside. He runs toward Mr. Miller's body, which is lying still across the bed, and places his fingers on the man's neck.

"Fuck!" the driver spits out and turns to me. "What have you done, bitch?"

I ignore him. For some reason, I can't take my eyes off the body on the bed. The eyes are still open, and even though I can't see them clearly, it seems like they are still looking directly at me. A slap lands on the side of my face.

"Wake the fuck up! We need to leave," the driver barks.

When I don't move, he grabs my arm and starts shaking me. A moment later, I feel the prick of a needle in my arm.

No!

That prick awakens whatever is left of my self-preservation. The pill bottle falls out of my hand. I pull my arm away, turn, and run out into the hallway.

It's well into the night and the inside of this place seems deserted. The two wide yellow stripes running the length of the carpet help me orient myself, and I follow them, running along several hallways in search of an exit. My vision clouds, and I'm becoming lightheaded. Every step I take is harder than the previous one, and it feels as if my legs are weighed down by concrete blocks. I turn the corner and keep running until I see a door at the end. There is a green-lit sign above it. I can't read the letters, but there is only one thing it could be. The exit.

As soon as I reach the door, I grab the knob and dash outside. It's a fire escape. I'm seeing double and my head spins, making me dizzier with each passing second, but I manage to grab the railing on the third try. Clutching the cold iron, I fumble down the steps, miraculously without falling. The moment my bare feet reach the ground, I turn left and run into a dark alley. A car horn blares on my right, and I turn just in time to see blinding lights shining into my face before the darkness swallows me.

 Pavel

"Shit!"

I open the car door and dash out, running to the front of my vehicle. On the road, barely a foot from the front bumper, lies a completely naked woman. I know I didn't hit her. I managed to stop the car before I reached her, but it looks like there is something wrong with her. Her body is shaking as if she has a high fever.

I bend and scoop her up into my arms. The smell of rancid male cologne invades my nostrils as I adjust my grip. The woman's skin is unusually cold and she is trembling so much that, if I wasn't clutching her to my chest, she'd slip from my grasp. Turning on my heel, I carry her to the car. Shifting her meager weight in my arms, I somehow manage to reach the handle and get the back door open. I don't have a blanket, so once I gently lower her onto the seat, I remove my jacket and drape it over the girl's naked body. She immediately curls into a fetal position while tremors continue to shake her slight form. As soon as I'm back behind the wheel, I hit speed dial on my phone, and floor the car.

"Doc!" I bark the moment he takes the call. "I have a girl in my car who seems to be having a seizure, maybe. Should I try to do something or drive straight to a hospital? Or should I bring her to you? I'm five minutes away."

"Symptoms?"

"She's shaking really bad, and her arms and hands are twitching." I throw a look over my shoulder. "Doesn't seem coherent."

"Foam at her mouth? Vomiting?"

I look over at the girl again. "No. Not at the moment."

"Bring her here," he says. "If she vomits, you need to stop the car and make sure she doesn't choke. It could be an epileptic seizure or an overdose."

"Okay." I toss the phone on the passenger seat.

Luckily, the traffic is light, so it takes me under five minutes to reach the building where the doc has a small clinic on the ground floor, just below his apartment. Since he mostly does house visits for the Bratva, he only uses it when someone needs an ultrasound or an x-ray.

I park at the front and lift the girl from the back seat. Her limbs are still twitching uncontrollably, but she's not vomiting. Holding her in my arms, still wrapped in my jacket, I run toward the glass door the doc is holding open.

"Put her on the gurney," he says and rushes toward the medical cabinet. "Why is she naked?"

"No idea. She ran out of a building, disoriented, and collapsed in the middle of the street. I almost hit her with my car."

The doc comes over carrying a syringe, leans over the girl, and pulls open her eyelid. "Overdose. Move away."

I take a couple of steps back and watch as he gives her an injection of something, then proceeds with attaching an IV with saline into her arm.

"I'll take a blood sample so we know what she's taken. But I won't have the results before tomorrow. I assume it was one of the common drugs so I've given her something to counteract it. It will reverse the effects." He grabs a blanket and places it over the girl. "Unless she is a heavy user, she should be okay in a couple of hours. Just drive her to a shelter or something and leave her for them to deal with."

I look down at the girl. Long dark brown strands are falling over her face, hiding it from view. She is still shaking under the blanket, but there is no twitching. Her breathing also sounds slightly better. What the fuck happened to her?

"I'll take her to my place for tonight," I say without taking my eyes off the girl. "When she's better in the morning, I'll take her home."

"Are you serious?"

"Yes." I look up and find Doc staring at me.

"You can't take a drug addict to your place."

"I won't drop her off at the shelter as if she's a bag of junk, Doc." One of the girl's arms is hanging down. I take her small hand and tuck it under the blanket next to her side. "And it will be just for tonight anyway."

The doc sighs and shakes his head. "If she is an addict,

which I'm pretty sure she is, she will go through withdrawal. With the medicine I gave her, it'll probably start right away. Depending on what she took and how heavy a user she is, it could take anywhere from a couple of days to two weeks for it to pass."

"Even though she is naked, her hair is clean, and her nails are manicured. It's more likely that someone drugged her while trying to sexually assault her, or she escaped an abusive partner."

The doc watches me, then nods. "All right. I'll see if I have a rape kit. I'll also do a basic exam. Wait outside."

I glance at the girl, who seems to be sleeping, and head toward the exit. It's started snowing. I lean back against the wall and stare at the street in front of me, wondering what the hell happened to that girl.

Fifteen minutes later, the doc comes out and stands next to me.

"So?" I ask.

He doesn't say anything at first, just peers into the night. "Doc?"

"They didn't 'try' to rape her," he says finally. "They demolished her, Pavel."

My head snaps to the side. "Explain."

"Someone tore into her; there is definitely evidence of forced trauma. Looks likes this may not have been the first time, either. She has older scar tissue. I took samples for STD tests and did a pregnancy test." He sighs and removes his glasses. "I've treated her the best I can, but she will need painkillers. I'll check if I have something nonaddictive she can take that won't react with the meds I gave her to reverse the overdose. She also has bruises, but they seem several days old. There is only one needle mark on her forearm, and it's fresh. They probably injected her with whatever she overdosed with."

"Send me the test results as soon as you get them," I say through gritted teeth.

"You're really taking her to your place?"

"Yes." I head back inside.

"Pavel," the doc calls after me. "I don't know what her mental state will be when she wakes up. Don't ask her what happened, just get her to her family. And tell them she'll need psychological help."

"Okay." I nod.

I sit down in the recliner and watch the sleeping girl curled up in the middle of my bed. At first, I thought about placing her in one of the other two bedrooms but decided against it. Better to be close in case her state worsens.

She seems better. Her breathing sounds normal, and the shaking stopped completely. I tilt my head, watching her small frame under the thick duvet. She's still naked under the covers. I didn't want to risk maneuvering her arms and legs to get her into one of my pajamas. What if she woke up and thought I was trying to hurt her?

I grip the sides of the recliner and draw a deep breath. What kind of sick bastard would abuse a woman in such a way? Especially someone so tiny. I close my eyes and try to subdue the urge to run to my car, drive back to where I found her, and search for the motherfucker who hurt her. I can't risk leaving her alone, though. What if she has another seizure? But I will find the man who dared beat and rape her, or whatever other torture the sick fuck subjected her to. And I will make him pay. My hold on the armrests intensifies, and the faint sound of wood squeaking follows. The sleeping girl stirs, and I release the recliner, not wanting to wake her.

I don't know what came over me and made me decide to bring her to my place. I could have easily left her at a hospital and told them to send me the bill for the services. It doesn't make sense, but I couldn't make myself leave her somewhere. It's been years since I felt any kind of connection with a person, even those closest to me. But seeing this girl, so hurt and unprotected, stirred something deep inside my soul. The need to shield her from anything that may try to hurt her again came viscerally, but with it, I also had the urge to destroy. It's strange to have this hunger for violence rising inside of me again after so many years.

The girl rolls to her other side, and one of her legs slips out from under the duvet. I get up and tuck it back under the covers.

She seems fine for the moment, sound asleep, so I decide to take a quick shower. Inside the walk-in closet on the other side of the room, I use the flashlight on my phone to find a pair of black pajama bottoms and boxer briefs. I'm already at the bathroom door when a thought surfaces, and I return to the closet to grab a T-shirt, as well. When I'm home, I usually wear just pajama bottoms, but the girl could get scared if she sees all the ink on my torso. She will probably be scared when she wakes up in a strange place, and there is no need to distress her more than necessary.

I turn the water to cold in the shower, hoping it'll help

me shake off the persistent urge to kill someone. It doesn't help much. Pressing my palms to the tiled wall, I lift my chin and let the cold spray hit me right in the face. As the freezing water runs down my body, I dig inside my brain, pulling out the memory of one of my last fights. The most violent one, since I need some way to deal with this urge to destroy someone. My opponent snuck a knife inside the ring and managed to slice my side twice before I overpowered him. I made sure he knew what I thought about his actions by breaking his back and burying his own blade to the hilt at the base of his skull. Violence isn't something I enjoy, but when I find myself in a beast's den, I inevitably become the very beast I'm fighting. It's nothing more than survival. Reliving that scene helps feed my thirst for destruction. Somewhat, at least.

I take no more than five minutes in the bathroom, so I expect the girl to still be sleeping soundly. Instead, she is tossing and turning in the bed, her body shaking. I rush over and press my palm to her forehead, finding it hot. She is mumbling something I can't decipher because her teeth are chattering too much. I bend my head trying to catch what she's saying.

"Cold . . ." her small voice whimpers. "So, so cold."

I grab the blanket folded at the foot of the bed, throw it over her, then take my phone from the nightstand.

"Doc," I say the moment he picks up, "the girl has a fever and is shaking like a leaf, saying she's cold."

"Withdrawal," he says. "It's a normal reaction."

"What can I do?"

"Nothing. Her body needs to go through that. She'll be better in a couple of hours. But it may happen again over the next few days. Make sure you tell the family that tomorrow."

"Okay. Anything else?"

"She will probably feel sick tomorrow, but she needs to drink liquids. Try giving her water the moment she wakes up," he says. "Oh, and Pavel, I probably don't have to tell you this, but it would be best if you don't touch her or get into her personal space. If she freaks out in the morning, give me a call and I'll go get Varya. She can stay with the girl until her family comes to pick her up."

"Thanks."

I lower the phone and observe the girl again. She is still shaking, but I don't think I should cover her with anything else. She'll get too hot. There's the mumbling again, but she's turned with her back to me so it's hard to hear. I put my knee on the bed and lean closer, trying to understand. She's crying. The whimpers are very low, broken, and that sound is so fucking heartbreaking.

The doc said I shouldn't try to touch her, but she's delirious now and probably doesn't know what's happening around her. I can't bear the idea of doing nothing any longer. I reach out and place my palm on her back, over the blanket, and brush it lightly. She doesn't pull away, so I sprawl down onto the bed behind her, making sure my body doesn't touch hers, and continue stroking her back. After some time, the crying stops. I pull my hand off, intending to get up when the girl suddenly turns around and buries her face into my chest. I lie there, not moving, not daring to touch her, but also unable to move away. Her hot breath fans my chest as she lies with her hands squeezed into fists and tucked between our bodies. She's still shaking.

A barely audible whisper reaches my ears. "More."

I look down at her, having no idea what she meant by that.

"Please."

The way she says it guts me. It's like a call for help from a drowning person. Slowly, I place my palm where I think the small of her back may be. I can't really tell with her bundled under the covers. I move my hand across her back, up then down. The girl sighs, snuggles closer, and buries her nose in the crook of my neck.

It must be dawn already, but I'm not certain because I pulled the heavy drapes over the windows. I should get some sleep. I have a meeting with the pakhan this afternoon, after which I'll be stuck at the club until at least three in the morning. Instead of doing what I'm sure the doc would advise—going to another room—I stay where I am, with a girl whose name I don't even know, and stroke her back until her breathing evens out and she falls asleep again.

CHAPTER
Two

THE DOOR ON THE OPPOSITE WALL IS HUGE AND IS made of the darkest wood I've ever seen. An hour must have passed since I woke up. I can't be sure, though. There's a clock on the wall, ticking, but it doesn't help because I can't see the details of the face or hands. Based on the sliver of light visible between the drapes, it must be midday.

I desperately need to pee, but I'm afraid to move from my spot in this bed. The last thing I remember is following the yellow hallway lines after I ran out of Mr. Miller's room and finding the door with the exit sign. I don't have a clue where I am. I don't know how I got here. And I have no idea what they are going to do with me. My body is shaking. The pain between my legs is still there but not as strong, and my head hurts as if it's going to explode. Other than that, I feel fine. Physically, at least. Mentally? Mentally, I feel fine, too. In fact, I feel great.

That can't be good.

The door opens and someone walks in, then stops abruptly. It's a man, that much I can discern even from this distance. He's tall and very muscular, wearing a black T-shirt and baggy black pants. His hair is either dark blond or light brown. That summarizes everything I can make out. I had a week left until my scheduled second eye surgery, but then . . . everything happened. The doctor said he expected to correct my nearsightedness almost entirely.

The man just stands there, and I wonder how long he plans on just staring at me.

"Good morning," he says finally, and a pleasant shiver passes down my body. I've never in my life met a man with a voice so deep. "How are you feeling?"

I squint my eyes, trying to see him better, but he's still just a blurred shape.

The man takes a tentative step forward. "Can you tell me your name?"

I can, but I don't feel like talking right now. I don't know why. I just don't. Another step. He's in the middle of the room now.

"Your family is probably worried about you. Can you give me their number to call them? So they can come to take you home?"

Yes, my brother and sister are probably going out of their minds. I've been missing for two months. Arturo must be feeling crazy with no information on me. He's been both a father and a mother to me and my sister since we were five. And Sienna, oh my God, I can't even think about it. I need to call them to let them know I'm okay.

Nausea claws its way into my throat. I don't want to call Arturo, because I'll have to tell him what happened. What I did. I don't want my family to know that their sister is a prostitute and an addict. They'll probably tell me everything will be okay. My body starts shaking. It's not going to be okay.

Nothing will ever be okay again.

"What's wrong?" the man asks and takes another step toward me.

They probably think I'm dead. Good. It's better that way. I'm not worth their worry. I'd never be able to look them in the eyes. The sister they knew doesn't exist anymore. She's gone. And in her place is this disgusting, filthy creature who lets people violate her and sell her body while she does nothing to stop it. Nothing! My teeth chatter and I can't breathe.

"Please, tell me what's wrong."

His voice is so calming. I should be scared shitless, having an unknown man here, considering what I've gone through. I'm not. The thing is, I had so many nasty things done to me that there is nothing he can do to hurt me. I'm more scared of Arturo and Sienna finding out than being violated again. I try breathing deeper but can't. I can only manage small gasps.

A hand enters my field of vision and I flinch, expecting him to hit me. Instead, the man takes the blanket that has fallen off my shoulders and wraps it around me. His palm rests on my back and slowly moves up and down. He did the same thing last night. I remember waking up and being freezing cold when a hand started comforting my back. It made me feel safe, something I thought I would never feel again. I did last night.

My eyes focus on the blanket wrapped around me because I can't look at him right now, but I can finally fill my lungs. I close my eyes, and a faint melody plays somewhere deep inside my mind. The notes are soft, barely recognizable, but still, my heart skips a beat. I thought I had lost my music. As the hand on my back continues its path, up then down and up again, the music gets a little louder. Beethoven's "Moonlight Sonata." Deep. Soothing. Just like his voice.

"I'm going to get you some water," the man says, and his hand vanishes off my back as he moves away.

I scream.

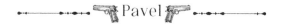 Pavel

I freeze. Did I accidentally touch her skin or do something to trigger her?

Careful not to touch her, I step away from the bed, but the girl suddenly leaps toward me. Her arms come around my neck, squeezing it in a vice-like grip, while her legs wrap around my waist. I stand next to the bed, stunned, with the girl clinging to me like a baby koala. She tucks her face into the crook of my neck and is humming something. Now what? Should I try putting her back on the bed? Or should I just wait until she decides to get down?

I wait for a couple of moments to see if she'll let me go, but she clings to me relentlessly. It looks like I'm stuck with her like this for now. Carefully, I wrap one arm around her back and lean to take the package of painkillers the doc gave me from the nightstand. I put the medicine in the pocket of my pajama bottoms and place my hand under her thigh. Since she is still completely naked, I pull the blanket off the bed and cover her body, tucking the ends under her chin.

"Let's go get you some water," I say and head out of the bedroom.

I carry the girl into the kitchen. She doesn't let go while I get a bottle of water from the fridge and walk toward the cupboard to take a glass. I do it with one hand since I'm still holding her with the other one, afraid she might slip and fall.

"Want to come down and drink your water?" I ask.

She squeezes her arms tighter around my neck. I look at the glass I placed on the counter, then at the bottle standing next to it. Okay. I have no fucking idea what to do.

"Listen, mishka, the doctor said you need to drink something. Please don't make me force you."

The arms around my neck tighten, then loosen, and I carefully put her down. The girl stands in front of me, clutching the blanket with her hands. Her head is bent down, hair has fallen on either side of her face, hiding it from view.

"Here." I pass her the glass of water and take the medicine out of my pocket.

The second I place the pills on the counter, the girl abruptly steps back.

"They're painkillers. Look." I take two pills from the bottle, throw them into my mouth, and offer one to her.

She stares at the pill on my palm, steps backward again, and bumps into the kitchen island.

"Okay." I put the pill and the bottle on the counter and hold the glass of water out to her. "Just water. All of it, please."

When she drinks the water and hands the glass back to me, I nod and take it. "Good. Do you want to take a shower?"

The girl doesn't reply.

There isn't much light in the kitchen. I usually keep all the blinds down during the day because that's when I sleep. I tilt my head to the side, trying to gauge the look on her face. She seems confused. I know she can speak, so I don't understand why she's not answering any of my questions.

"Do you want to shower?" I try again.

She bites her lower lip and something close to frustration passes across her face, but she doesn't reply. Not even a nod. What am I going to do with her? There is mud on her right shoulder and arm, and some in her hair. Probably from when she fell on the street.

"All right, I'll take you to get a shower. Nod, mishka."

An exhale leaves the girl's lips, and she nods. I turn toward my bedroom, but immediately feel a tug on my T-shirt and throw a look over my shoulder. The girl is right behind me, holding the blanket with one hand and clutching the hem of my T-shirt in the other.

She follows me across the living room and into my bedroom, hanging on to my shirt all the way. When we reach the bathroom, I nod toward the cabinet on the right. "You'll find towels and some basic toiletries there."

The girl remains behind me, still gripping my shirt. I turn to leave, but a low whimper stops me in my tracks. When I look over my shoulder, I find the girl with her lips pressed tightly together and her eyes wide and searching my face.

"Want me to stay?" I ask.

She doesn't reply. Not that I expected her to. But her eyes peeking between the tangled dark strands and boring into mine say enough. Without thinking, I reach out to sweep the hair off her face, but abruptly pull my hand away when I realize what I'm doing.

"All right. I'll wait here." I face the door. "Let me know when you're done."

Nothing happens at first, but a couple of moments later she releases my T-shirt. I hear her pee and flush the toilet. The shower turns on shortly after.

I stare at the door in front of me, thinking. I'm no expert on mental health, but I know that her behavior is way off. It seems the total opposite of what I would expect from a woman who's experienced sexual assault. I assumed she wouldn't want to go within a ten-foot radius of an unknown man. I didn't expect this, and I'm not sure how to behave.

A sound of rapid breathing, like she's hyperventilating, reaches me. "Is everything okay?" I ask over my shoulder without looking toward the shower.

There is a sniff and more heavy breathing. I finally look inside the stall and see the girl sitting on the floor with the blanket still wrapped around her. She is frantically scrubbing the washcloth over the inside of her legs. The skin there is so red, it looks raw.

"Fuck." I dash across the bathroom, get into the shower, and crouch in front of her. "That's enough. You're clean." I take her hand and untangle her fingers from the washcloth. Almost reluctantly she lets it go, loosening her hold on the blanket at the same time. The wet mass falls off her shoulders. "It's okay."

The overhead spray is scorching hot as it rains down on us, but her body is shaking. I scoop her into my arms and step toward the bathroom vanity, carefully setting her down on the counter. The towel I used earlier is hanging on the wall next to me. I grab it and wrap it around her shoulders.

"Mishka, look at me," I say and grasp her chin between my fingers to tilt her head up. "I need to take off my T-shirt or I'll get you wet again."

My clothes are completely soaked, but I don't think it's a good idea to leave her here alone while I go to change.

"Is that okay?" I ask.

Her red-rimmed eyes regard me, and they're darting back and forth as if she wants to say something, but her lips remain sealed. Then, she parts them and sucks in a small breath, followed by the sound of her chattering teeth. The harsh LED light above the sink is shining directly onto her. I look over her small body wrapped in my towel and the dark brown hair hanging down around her face. I haven't had the opportunity to see her that well until now, and it strikes me how young she looks.

"Christ, baby. How old are you?" I whisper.

And, of course, there is no answer.

I grab a handful of the material of my T-shirt at my back and pull it over my head, dropping it to the floor. "Don't be scared. They're just tattoos," I say.

The girl's gaze moves to my torso as she takes in the multitude of grotesque scenes covering my skin. She squints and leans forward, examining the black shapes. Her gaze travels upward until her face is right in front of mine, two brown eyes staring me down.

"Can you please say something?" I ask. "Your name?"

Nothing.

"I'm Pavel. But people usually call me Pasha. It's a Russian nickname."

Her eyes widen at that, but she doesn't utter a word.

"Okay. Let's take you to bed and get you warm."

The moment the words leave my mouth, she clings to me again, wrapping her arms and legs as before. I pick up the towel that fell next to the sink, put it around her shoulders, and carry her to my bed.

"I need to change," I say as I cover the girl with a blanket. "I'll get you something to wear, too. Is a T-shirt okay?"

I don't know why I keep asking her questions when she never replies. After I have her tucked into bed, I cross the room and enter my walk-in closet. I change into dry pajama pants and put on another T-shirt, then I rummage around trying to find a smaller T-shirt. I know I have one that Kostya gave me a couple of years ago which was several sizes too small. He had it custom ordered with "Classy but Anal" printed on the front. Idiot.

There's a shuffling sound, and I look over my shoulder to find the girl standing in the doorway, with the blanket wrapped around her. She takes a step inside and looks at the shelf where I keep my T-shirts. There aren't that many, maybe ten in total. I only wear them when I work out. The rest of my wardrobe consists of underwear, pajama bottoms, dress shirts, and suits. I don't own any jeans, sweatshirts, or other casual clothes. I swore to myself years ago that I would never wear jeans again.

Her gaze falls to the bottom shelf where I keep my shoes, then shifts to the right where a rack runs the length of the space. There are at least thirty suits and twice that number of shirts hanging off it. The moment she sees this, she stiffens, takes two steps back, and dashes away.

I grab the first T-shirt off the shelf and exit the closet, finding the girl curled up on the bed with her back toward me.

"I'll leave this for you here," I say and put the folded shirt at the foot of the bed. She doesn't react.

I should get her something to eat, but it can wait. She needs sleep more. I take a seat on the edge of the bed, watching her small form. The edge of the blanket is pulled up all the way to her forehead. I reach out to place my hand on her back, over the blanket, and stroke it. She releases a small sigh and relaxes slightly under my palm. She's all the way on the other side of the bed, so I climb up and lie down a safe distance from her, and resume soothing her back.

Something warm presses into my side. I open my eyes and find the girl snuggled into me with her arm thrown over my chest and her face pressed to my upper arm. Seems like we both fell asleep. The clock on the wall across the room shows four p.m. Shit.

As carefully as possible, I untangle myself from the sleeping girl and head into the bathroom to get myself ready for work. When I emerge fifteen minutes later, she is still asleep. I consider waking her to let her know I have to leave but decide not to disturb her.

There isn't much in the kitchen or fridge because I usually order food or eat at work. I find some eggs, a loaf of bread and some marmalade, and place it all on the counter for her. With that done, I scribe a quick note saying I've gone to work and she should eat. Then, I leave it on the nightstand next to the bed. The blanket has slid from her body, so I cover her again, but instead of leaving right away, I watch her for several long moments.

Asya

Cold. So cold. I wrap the blanket tightly around myself and sit up in bed. There's no one around. Where is he? Maybe he's in another room. I listen for sounds, any sounds, but there is only silence. The floor lamp next to the bed is on, throwing light on a piece of paper lying on the nightstand. I take it and bring it closer to my face. I've been nearsighted all my life; I need to hold the note a foot in front of my eyes to be able to clearly make out the writing.

The note says he won't be back before late tonight. I put the paper back on the nightstand. He left me alone in his apartment. I shudder and wrap the blanket tighter around me. What time is it? How long will I have to wait until he's back? I scoot back in the bed until I'm huddled in the corner, wedged between the headboard and the wall, and close my eyes.

What the fuck is going on with me? When I woke up this morning, I felt completely fine until he mentioned my family. Just the idea of them finding out what happened to me made me lose it. It was as if I was suddenly thrown into a black abyss. The darkness is too familiar. It was the same void where I spent the last two months, completely detached from everything happening around me. Or to me. It felt like it would swallow me whole. Like invisible, poisonous gas, its toxic whisp encircled my mind, wanting me to let it inside. *Dirty*, it whispered. *Filthy. No one will ever want to touch you again.* But then, Pasha stroked my back. He didn't find me repulsive. The voices stopped, and the black hole closed.

I'm left with this strange conviction that it won't come back while he's nearby. But he's not here now.

When your brother finds out what happened, he'll be disgusted, the voice whispers in my ear. *He won't love you anymore. No one can love such a miserable creature. Letting strangers fuck you, while you did nothing to fight back. Repulsive.*

I breathe slowly in and out, trying to block it out. It doesn't work.

It's all your fault. You brought this onto yourself. It was your decision to go with that guy.

I drag my hands into my hair and squeeze as if pulling at the roots will rip the voice out of my head. But it continues.

You thought he was nice. He was a sexual predator who raped you and threw you into a prostitution ring, and you found him nice! You're not capable of sound reasoning.

I reach out to grab the note Pasha left and focus on the first couple of lines.

"When you wake up, you can explore the apartment. I left some food on the counter in the kitchen. Eat."

It's an instruction. Not a question. I don't have to make the decision myself. I just need to follow what he said. A sigh of relief leaves my lips. Clutching the note in my hand, I climb down off the bed and, taking the T-shirt he left, head out of the room.

Pasha's place is very upscale. Everything—from the modern dark furniture to the soft, thick carpets and heavy curtains—looks expensive. There is no clutter, no little trinkets on the shelves, or anything like that. I found two other

37

bedrooms, significantly smaller than the one where I slept. They don't seem to be in use.

The living room is the largest space in the apartment, with a TV mounted on the wall and a couch and two recliners in front of it. I stand in the middle of the room and look around. One bookshelf. Several modern paintings on the walls. It's nice, but it all seems staged as if it's a setup for an interior design magazine or a showroom. It feels strange to be in a place like this.

At home, all our shelves and walls are covered with photos of Sienna and me, with a random one of Arturo when we managed to convince him to take a picture with us. Sienna's fashion magazines and my music sheets are strewn around. The throw pillows on the sofa are mismatched. There are dog toys everywhere. Random hair products and body balms usually litter strange places like the kitchen counter or the TV shelf. Something squeezes in my chest when I think about home. It seems foreign, somehow, as if my home belongs to someone else.

I clench the paper in my hand tighter and head into the kitchen. The countertops are shiny and black, with a glass stove that looks like it has never been used. The size of the black fridge seems like it could store enough food to last ten people a week, but when I open it, the only contents are several bottles of water, a carton of milk, three tomatoes, and an unopened pack of cheese.

The countertop runs the entire length of the wall, but the only item on it is a coffee machine. No spice jars, no holder for cups. Nothing. Just a coffee machine. On the island, he left out some breakfast food for me. Should I cook some eggs, or just have some marmalade on the bread? An unpleasant tingling spreads through my insides. It's either eggs or marmalade; I don't think I can eat both. But when I think about picking one, the anxiety in my stomach intensifies.

What the fuck is wrong with me that I can't make such an idiotically small decision? The same thing happened this morning when Pasha asked me if I wanted to take a shower. I was filthy. I needed a shower. But when he asked, I couldn't make the decision. I grab the edge of the island and stare at the stuff left out for me. Eggs or marmalade? It's a simple choice, damn it! Why can't I fucking decide?!

After twenty minutes of staring, I end up frying the eggs while eating a slice of bread with marmalade and feeling like an idiot the whole time.

At least the fever I had has passed.

By the time I'm finished with my meal, it's already dark outside, and I don't know what to do. The note said to explore and eat. Not what to do after that. I could go back to sleep or maybe read something. There is a bunch of books on the bookshelf in the living room. I can't watch TV without my glasses unless I stand right in front of it. Read? Sleep? I need to make a decision again, but I can't!

Grabbing the sides of my head, I pull on my hair and a frustrated whine leaves my lips. I read the last part of the note again.

"I went to work and won't be back till 3 a.m. If you're thinking of running away, please don't. Wait until I'm back."

He said to wait for him. Simple. Direct. Unquestionable. The pressure in my chest dissipates. I stand a couple of steps from the front door. And wait. Anyone looking at me now might think they are seeing a trained dog. I don't give a fuck. The only thing I care about at this moment is not feeling this overwhelming anxiety anymore. I'll deal with my fucked-up psyche some other day. I sit on the floor, wrap my arms around my legs, and stare at the front door.

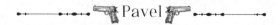

Pavel

My phone rings as I'm parking my car at the end of the long row of vehicles pulled up in front of the pakhan's house. The last in line is a big red bike. Something major must be up since Roman's called the top brass, including Sergei. I grab the phone from the passenger seat and take the call.

"Doc?"

"I have the girl's results. As far as STDs are concerned, she's clean. Negative on the pregnancy, too. The bloodwork shows she's a bit anemic, but that's it."

"What about the drugs?"

"Well, that's the interesting part. The substance found in her system isn't listed. It looks like it may be something new, something that hasn't hit the mainstream, yet."

"That's strange."

"Wait, there's more. The test came back on the pills Vladimir dropped off the other day. It's the same stuff."

"Are you sure?"

"Yes."

"Did you tell Roman?"

"I did. Just got off from the call with him."

I stiffen. "So . . . you told him about the girl?"

"Of course. Why? Should I not have?"

"Nope, just asking," I say and squeeze the steering wheel

until my knuckles go white. The fact that he told Roman about the girl doesn't sit well with me, and that doesn't make sense. I've never felt the need to hide anything from the pakhan.

"How is she?" the doc continues. "Did her family come to get her?"

"She's still at my place."

"What? Why didn't you call her parents or someone?"

"She won't talk. In fact, she hasn't said a word."

"Shit. She must be scared shitless. We should have had Varya stay with her until her family is able to come. You should probably stay away while she's there."

"About that." I rub my neck. "She doesn't seem scared of me. She's actually been glued to my side since the moment she woke up this morning. Won't let me leave her sight. She even insisted I stay in the bathroom while she took a shower."

"Hmm. This isn't my specialty, but I do know that assault victims can react in multiple ways. Does she flinch when you come close?"

"When I tried to leave the room to get her a glass of water, she screamed and jumped into my arms. Naked," I say. "Do you have any advice on what I should do? How to behave until I can reach her family?"

"No idea. I'm not a psychologist. But, I'll make a few calls and let you know what I find out."

"Thanks, Doc."

I put the phone in my jacket and look down at my watch. I shouldn't have left her alone, but all this is new to me. I've never had anyone to worry about. Never had to take care of someone. And no one ever took care of me, so I haven't a clue what I'm doing.

As I assumed, almost everyone from the Bratva's top circle is here.

The head of security, Dimitri, is standing next to Roman's desk, while Mikhail is sitting in the chair near the window. Mikhail oversees the transport operations involving the Bratva's drug products, and he's also in charge of information extraction. In other words—torture, when necessary. Sergei, the pakhan's half brother, is leaning on the wall beside the door, flipping a knife blade in his hands. He handles the negotiations with our suppliers and buyers. And kills them occasionally.

"Fyodor's daughter, Ruslana, has been found dead," Maxim, the second in command, says and places a yellow folder in front of Roman. "The body was found in a dumpster in the suburbs. Some homeless man stumbled upon it."

"Cause of death?" Roman asks.

"Suspected overdose."

"Ruslana was a good kid. Sophomore in college. It doesn't sound like her to get mixed up with drugs." Roman nods toward the folder. "When did she go missing?"

"Last month. Her father said she went to a store and never came back."

"Did he file a missing person's report?"

"Yes. Nothing came of it. It was as if she fell off the earth. But that's not the strangest thing." Maxim takes a piece of paper out of the folder and passes it to Roman. "Here's the medical examiner's report. She was high on heroin, but they also found traces of an unidentified substance. I pulled some strings and had the results cross-checked against the pills taken from the dealer at Ural. Same thing."

After a brief scan of the contents, Roman asks. "You think the heroin is a cover-up?"

"Probably." He nods.

"Drugs are not ice cream. You can't just whip up a new flavor in someone's kitchen." Roman drums his fingers on the desk and looks at Mikhail who is sitting to my right. "Did you get anything from the dealer Pavel caught?"

"He just kept repeating what he told Pasha," Mikhail says. "A friend gave him the pills in exchange for debt forgiveness. He didn't know how his friend got the drugs or what they were. We have nothing, just the name of this friend. But, it seems his buddy has disappeared. Yuri has men keeping their eyes on his place. As soon as he surfaces, they will bring him in."

I watched Mikhail work over a guy once a few years back. He made torture into an art form. If Mikhail couldn't extract anything else from the dealer, it means there wasn't anything left.

Roman sets the folder aside and leans forward, placing his elbows on the desk. "Now, onto the second issue. What the fuck is wrong with you all—collecting random unconscious women and taking them home with you?"

All heads turn toward Sergei who is sitting on my right.

"Oh, don't look at me!" He laughs, "I got mine years ago and I'm done."

"And don't we all remember the monumental fuckup that resulted in?" Roman snaps. "The speculations are still rampant all over Mexico about what happened to the Sandoval compound. Some people don't believe the bullshit that the

43

government is pushing about it being an earthquake, and think it was a meteorite strike instead."

"Well, since Pasha doesn't know shit about explosives, I'd say we're good." Sergei smirks at me. "Wanna share something about the girl Roman told me you have at home?"

Everyone's attention immediately switches to me.

"I have no idea who she is. She won't talk," I say. "But when I found her, she was spiked with the same crap that was being peddled at Ural."

"I need updates on this new drug," Roman says. "I want to know who's making it and for what purpose. And I want them dealt with. Fyodor's daughter was a good kid. Everyone who was in any way involved in her death will pay for it. In blood."

He jerks his head toward the door, which means the meeting is over. Kostya and Mikhail leave the office first, and the rest of us follow.

I'm crossing the foyer toward the front door when I hear high-pitched, female screams. I turn around, spotting Kostya cowering in the corner, protectively holding his hands over his head. Olga and Valentina have him pinned, crying and hitting him with kitchen rags. Looks like they still haven't gotten over the fact that he broke up with both of them. The poor bastard had to move out of the mansion on the same day he told them they were done to avoid bodily harm. I leave Kostya to his misery and head outside.

My phone rings as I'm getting into my car. It's the doc.

"Where are you?"

"Just leaving the pakhan's house, heading to Ural," I say. "Why?"

"I just spoke with a friend who's a psychologist. She often

44

works with assault victims. I explained the situation to her and told her about the girl's behavior."

"And?" I switch the phone to hands-free and put the car in reverse. "Did she have any idea what's going on?"

"She wasn't surprised and surmised that the girl has developed an attachment to you," he says. "Apparently, some assault victims tend to stay away from men. Especially strangers, but sometimes even family members. Others, however, form a strong bond to whomever has saved them. They latch onto their protector, even if it's a male."

"I don't understand," I say.

"The trauma of being sexually assaulted is an experience filled with violence. It transforms a person's sense of safety, the way they look at the world, and their relationships with other people. Looks like this girl started to associate the feeling of safety with you. She sees the rest of the world as unsafe. As her savior, you've become her 'safe place.'"

"I didn't save her. She saved herself. Ran out of that building."

"Realistically speaking, yes. But in her eyes, you're the one who saved her. We don't know how long she was held captive and sexually assaulted. You taking her to your place could be the first time she's felt safe in days. Weeks. Maybe months."

"Jesus fuck."

"Go home. Talk to her. She needs professional help, and she needs her family," he says in a grave voice. "And she shouldn't be left alone."

As soon as I cut the connection, I call Ivan and send him to Ural. It's an hour-long drive from Roman's to my place, and the whole time I mull over what the doc had said. I should have stayed with the girl. What if she woke up and was scared because I was gone? No one in their right mind would have left the girl in that state alone in a strange place. I wasn't thinking.

I hit the steering wheel with my hand and press the gas pedal harder.

When I open the front door, it's pitch black inside. Could she still be sleeping? I reach for the switch, turn on the lights, and stop dead in my tracks. The girl is sitting on the floor a few paces from the door with her arms wrapped around her legs. Her body is shaking uncontrollably.

"Shit." I crouch down beside her, intending to scoop her up, but as soon as I reach for her, she leaps into my arms. Wrapping herself around me like a koala bear again, she buries her face in the crook of my neck.

Holding on under her thighs, I carry the girl to my bedroom. My intention to gently lower her onto the bed doesn't go as planned when her arms and legs squeeze me in a tight hold.

"I'm so sorry for leaving you alone," I whisper and sit down on the edge of the bed.

There is a bundled blanket next to me, so I reach for it and wrap it around the girl's shoulders. She doesn't move, just clings onto me, still shaking.

"You're safe." I place my hand on her nape and stroke her back with my other one in what I hope is a soothing motion. "You're safe."

A small sigh leaves her lips, and her body relaxes in my

arms. I keep up my comforting strokes for at least half an hour before she lifts her head off my shoulder. I reach for the lamp next to the nightstand, turning the dimmer switch to bring up the lights a bit more. The girl blinks a couple of times, probably adjusting to the sudden brightness, then looks right into my eyes.

"Feeling better?" I ask.

She doesn't reply, just stares at my face for a couple of seconds. Dear God, she is so damn young. She uncoils her arms from around my neck and trails her hands over my shoulders and down my chest, stopping at the lapels of my suit jacket. Her eyes snap down to where her hands are, and her body suddenly goes rigid. I follow her gaze and see that it's focused on my tie. She starts shaking again and a whimper leaves her lips.

"What's wrong?"

The girl's breathing becomes faster and shallower, and her eyes keep staring at my tie in horror.

"Look at me." I cup her face with my palms and tilt her head up until our gazes connect. There's panic in her dark brown eyes. "Good. Now, breathe."

She tries, but her breath hitches. Another try. Her lower lip trembles, and I hear a soft whisper but can't make out what she's saying.

"I didn't hear you, baby. Can you try again?"

She closes her eyes and leans forward. Her words are faint next to my ear, "They always . . . wore suits."

It takes me a few seconds to understand what she's referring to. The moment I do, a cold chill runs down my spine. She said "they." Plural. I thought she may have been in an abusive relationship with some psycho who drugged her.

I let go of her face and quickly remove my jacket,

47

throwing it toward the middle of the room where she won't see it. Then, I start undoing my tie. The girl looks down, her gaze locking onto my hands as I'm pulling at the knot, and the shaking in her body intensifies.

"Look at me." I manage to form the words, speaking evenly so I don't frighten her. It's difficult because the anger raging inside of me is threatening to erupt. "Look at my eyes. Good girl. I'm throwing it away, okay?" I let the tie fall to the floor.

The moment the tie is out of view, her body relaxes a bit, but she's still shaking.

"Shirt as well?" I ask, and without waiting for the answer, I start on the buttons.

The girl bites her lower lip and nods.

"Okay, baby." I undo the last button and yank off the shirt. "Better?"

I stare into her red-rimmed eyes, and God, she seems so lost. She looks down again and slowly places her hand on my naked chest. The tip of her finger moves across my collarbone where my tattoos start, then slowly traces downward. It's a barely there touch, outlining the shapes inked on my skin.

"I'm afraid I can't remove these, mishka," I say.

Her eyes lift back to mine, and as she watches me, the corners of her lips curve upward ever so slightly.

"Is that a smile?"

She shrugs.

It was a tiny smile, but a smile nevertheless. It completely transforms her face, giving me a glimpse of the woman she was before everything that happened to her.

"What's your name, baby?"

The need to know her name, the tiniest of details about her, has been eating me alive.

"It's Asya," she says in a small voice. Unusual name.

"Asya," I try it out. It fits her. "It's a very pretty name. And your last name?"

"DeVille," she whispers.

I raise my eyebrows. "You're Italian?"

She nods.

The last name sounds familiar, but I can't place it. "Are you from Chicago?"

"New York."

The moment she says it, the realization comes. "Are you related to Arturo DeVille?"

"He's my brother." She bites her lip. "You know Arturo?"

The underboss of the New York Cosa Nostra Family. Shit. I haven't met Arturo DeVille, but Roman always makes sure the Bratva has intel on each and every person connected to us in any way.

"I'm a member of the Russian Bratva, mishka. Your don's wife is the sister to the wife of one of our enforcers," I say. "We need to call your brother right away and let him know you're here."

Asya's body goes stone-still. "Please . . . don't."

"Why?" I ask as nausea suddenly comes over me. "Does he have something to do with what happened to you?"

She shakes her head, then wraps her arms around my neck and snuggles into my chest. "He probably thinks I'm dead. I want to keep it that way."

"But, he's your brother. He's probably going nuts with worry." I pass my hand through her dark brown strands. "You need to tell him you're okay."

"I'm not fucking okay!" she snaps, then climbs down off my lap and pins me with her gaze. "Those people have been pumping me full of drugs and selling my body for months. And I let them! I did nothing! What kind of pitiful being just lets that happen without fighting back?"

She's crying while yelling. And I let her. Anger is good. Any kind of reaction is good. So, I don't make a move. Don't try to calm her down. I just sit on the edge of the bed and watch her in silence.

"Do you know that last night, when you found me, was the first time I tried to run away?" she continues. "You want me to tell my brother that? He raised me better than to be a fucking doormat! I would rather never see him again than have him learn what I allowed them to turn me into!"

She takes a deep breath and grabs my shirt off the floor near her feet. Stepping onto the edge of it she uses both hands to pull on the material, throwing her whole weight into her task, until the shirt rips. Then, she starts shredding it. I watch her in amazement. I thought she was meek and delicate, but as I observe her glorious rage, I realize how very wrong I was. There is fire in her and fierce life. The people who hurt her, who broke her spirit—they haven't banished it completely. And I will find every single one of them and make them pay.

"I hate them! I hate them so much!" she roars and looks up at me. "And you? Why the fuck are you just sitting there? How can you simply be watching me have a mental break-down and do nothing?" She throws a torn piece of material in my face and screams in frustration when I don't make a move. "What the fuck is wrong with you?" She places her hands on my chest and shoves me. "Shouldn't you try to calm me down?"

"No," I say.

"No? You'll just watch me fall apart?" she shoves at me again. Then one more time.

"You're not falling apart, Asya." I reach out and trace the line of her chin with my thumb. "You're pulling yourself together."

"Pulling together?" Her eyes widen, and she bursts into a fit of hysteric laughter. "When I woke up, I couldn't decide if I should eat the eggs or marmalade! I couldn't make the most basic decision. I spent twenty minutes staring at the stuff you left out on the counter and had to eat both because I couldn't choose!"

The last words get lost in a fit of crying. Her shoulders sag and she looks down at her bare feet. Placing my forefinger under her chin, I tilt her head up until our eyes meet.

"What do you want?" I ask.

She blinks at me, and two tears slide down her cheeks.

"Do you want them dead?"

There is a sharp intake of breath, but she doesn't reply. I reformulate my question into a statement.

"You want them dead."

Squeezing her lips tightly together, she nods.

"They will die," I say. "What else do you want?"

No reply.

"You don't want your family to see you like this."

Another nod.

"I'll never be the person I was before," she whispers.

"No. You won't." I lightly pinch her chin. "And that's okay. They'll love you just the same. What happened to you, changed you, Asya. It would change anyone. Irrevocably. You need to accept the person you've become. You're still you.

Changed, yes, but that shouldn't keep you from the people who care about you."

She sniffs and climbs back onto my lap. Again her limbs wrap around me, and she buries her face in the crook of my neck. Barely audible murmurs escape her lips, and I tilt my head to the side to hear her better. Once she's done, I stare at the far bedroom wall for a long time, thinking about what she just asked of me.

If Roman finds out, it won't end well. We've been maintaining a good relationship with the Cosa Nostra, but if I let her stay, it may mean war. And if Asya's brother finds out, he will probably kill me.

I inhale and nod. "Okay, mishka. You can stay."

CHAPTER
Three

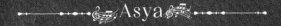 Asya

"I s marmalade okay?" Pasha asks and places the jar on the counter.

I grip the hem of his T-shirt harder as he turns to face me.

"I don't have anything else here, but I'll run to the store later and buy more food. I rarely eat at home. We'll order some clothes for you, too."

I tilt my head up and find him watching me. "Thank you."

I'm wearing another of his T-shirts with nothing underneath. No panties. No bra, either. It feels strange.

When I woke up this morning, I had a fever again. Pasha wrapped me in a blanket and pulled me against his chest. We lay in his bed for what felt like hours until my body finally stopped shaking. He carried me into the bathroom and stayed there while I did my business and took a shower. After I brushed my teeth, he wrapped me in a fluffy towel and led me back to bed, where I waited with my eyes glued to the bathroom door while he had a shower.

"Do you want coffee?"

I look at the coffee machine, feeling like the most pathetic being on earth. "I don't know."

Pasha's palm gently presses against my back, moving up and down in a soothing motion. I take a deep breath and look up to find him watching me. There is no reluctance in his eyes. No reproach. And no pity.

"Did you drink coffee before?"

"No," I whisper.

"How about tea? I have chamomile, I think." He opens the cupboard, takes out a metal container and places it in front of me.

I just stare at it.

He lifts my chin with his finger. "Did you like drinking tea, Asya?"

"Yes."

"Let's assume you still do." He smiles, and it's so beautiful. "What did you like to eat for breakfast before?"

"Cereal with raisins," I say. "Sometimes, I'd have some with chocolate chunks instead."

"Then I'll buy a few of those. How about other food? What were your favorite dishes? Were you allergic to anything?"

I sniff, trying to stifle the urge to cry. He's asking the questions in a way that makes it easier for me to answer. He's not asking me to pick, which would raise my anxiety, but rather asking me about facts.

"I never liked broccoli or green peas. Everything else was okay with me," I say. "No food allergies."

"Did you prefer ordering takeout or cooking for yourself?"

"I liked cooking."

He nods. "Make me a list of ingredients, and I'll go to the grocery store tomorrow. We'll order something to eat today, but tomorrow, you can prepare one of your dishes."

I bite my lower lip. That would require picking one of many.

"How about lasagna for tomorrow? I don't think I've ever tried one. Did you like making lasagna?"

The weight pressing on my chest dissipates. I nod.

"Good. I'll go get my phone so you can make that list for me, but first, let's have some breakfast. Okay?"

"Okay."

I follow him around the kitchen as he puts the kettle on to boil and takes out the bread. He spreads the marmalade methodically, making sure it's evenly distributed over the whole slice.

There is a multitude of small scars that cover his knuckles. His hands and fully inked arms seem at odds with the posh, almost clinically impeccable surroundings. I take the opportunity to inspect his face a bit better, including his strong jaw and sharp cheekbones, noticing a few scars on his forehead and several more on his chin, too. Finally, I peer at his eyes. I can't make out their color, however, since he towers over me by at least a foot.

Pasha stops what he's doing and looks down at me. Why are his eyes so sad? I let go of his T-shirt and place my palm over his forearm. The muscles under my fingers tense, and I expect him to pull away, but he doesn't.

I tighten my hold on him and lean into his side to get closer to the warmth of his big body. The faint sound of music reaches me. Someone, a neighbor probably, must have turned the TV too loud, and without thinking about it, I hum along to the tune.

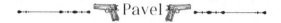

Pavel

Asya is bundled under the covers. I gave her an extra blanket when she wouldn't stop shivering earlier. She is asleep now, while I'm still awake, listening to her breathing.

She was okay this morning, but after lunch she got sick, and we barely managed to get to the bathroom in time. I held her hair while she emptied her stomach into the toilet, then helped her brush her teeth and carried her to the bed. Her fever spiked again, but it wasn't as bad as it was the first time. I don't have a thermometer, so I kept pressing the back of my hand to her forehead every five minutes, but it seemed like her temperature was only slightly elevated. The fever broke an hour ago, and she finally stopped tossing in bed.

I reach for my phone on the nightstand and type a message to Kostya, asking about the situation at the clubs. A minute later, I receive the reply—a bunch of Russian curses and wishes for my slow and painful demise. Apparently, he's not happy about having to fill in for me.

When I called the pakhan earlier today and asked for a few days off, I suggested having Ivan take over. Roman laughed and said he'd give the clubs to Kostya because it was time for him to start doing actual work instead of only chasing women and burning rubber on a regular basis.

Kostya started working alongside his brother, helping with the Bratva finances when he was barely twenty, but he's always been a problem child. Roman has a soft spot for him, though, since Kostya's the youngest in the inner circle. I guess we all do. Kostya is like everyone's little brother, and he shamelessly uses that to his advantage, constantly getting off the hook because of his age. Hopefully, he won't get any crazy ideas while he's filling in for me. If he decides to transform my clubs into strip clubs, I'm going to strangle him.

Asya stirs next to me, and I quickly feel her forehead. No fever, thank fuck. When I pull my fingers away, she grabs my hand and lays it on her chest. It looks like I'll be sleeping in the same bed with her again. I sprawl out next to her and watch her face. I kind of understand her reasoning for not letting me call her brother, but then again, I don't understand it at all. Wouldn't it be easier for her to be back home with her family? I've never experienced family dynamics, but I'm sure her brother and sister would do a much better job than me.

I reach out and turn off the lamp, closing my eyes. But sleep evades me. How did Asya end up in Chicago? Who are the people who took and kept her? Is there a connection to Fyodor's daughter? I have so many questions and zero answers.

Tilting my head to the side, I watch Asya's sleeping form. She's still clutching my hand in her own. I need to buy groceries first thing in the morning. I can't have her eat bread and marmalade three days in a row. I need to get some toiletries for her, as well. And clothes. But I kinda like her in my T-shirts.

A brown strand of hair has fallen over her face, so I reach out and carefully move it. Why did I let her stay?

CHAPTER
four

Pavel

I STAND IN FRONT OF THE BATHROOM MIRROR. GRAY jeans and a black T-shirt are lying folded on the counter next to the sink. They disgust me. I don't recall how long it's been since I've worn jeans, probably more than a decade.

It's not the garments themselves that are the problem, but rather the memories of digging through heaps of discarded clothes, mostly jeans, trying to find something that fit. Everything was always torn and dirty, and I didn't have the money for laundry before putting them on. People avoided me when I took the subway, making my shame nearly palpable.

The moment I started earning serious money through underground fights, I traded in my entire secondhand wardrobe for slacks and dress shirts. Eventually, I switched to suits. As time went on, I switched to more upscale clothes and added expensive watches and other accessories. It was all a means to forgetting what I had been for the first twenty years of my life. Trash. Someone from whom people would quickly turn away, ignoring my presence. The funny thing is, even though it has been nearly fifteen years, I can still smell the stench, whether from the clothes or the half-rotten food I dug out of the dumpsters in alleys behind restaurants, that always surrounded me.

I look at my face in the mirror, regarding the small scars scattered across my temples, the bridge of my nose, and my chin. They are faded now, barely noticeable, but I can still recall the fights that left me with each mark. I'm not even sure how many times my nose has been broken. Seven? Probably more.

I was barely eighteen when I started fighting for money. At first, it was a way to put food in my mouth, but as time passed, it transformed into something else. The people who came to watch, who chanted my name . . . they fed the deep yearning I've always felt in my soul. The need to belong. Somewhere. Anywhere. The excitement of the crowd as it cheered for me, made me feel less alone.

I'm not exactly sure why I said yes when Yuri approached me after one of my fights and offered me a position in the Bratva. Maybe I wanted to feel closer to my heritage. There weren't any Russian kids in the foster homes when I was growing up. By the time I aged out of the system, I had almost forgotten my mother tongue. Years with the Bratva helped me regain it, so I have no trouble with the language anymore. But it's not the same. It no longer feels like my first language, but neither does English.

I trace the more prominent scar on the left side of my jaw with my index finger. No matter how hard I try to hide the past, some reminders, visible or not, will always remain.

Is that why I let Asya stay? Maybe, I recognized a kindred spirit trying to outrun the past and wanted to help. After all, I know how it feels to not have anyone to turn to. But I'm afraid that it's only part of the reason. My true motivation is much, much more selfish. I've been alone all my life and have gotten used to it. It's the way I function. But after Asya stumbled onto my path, I realized how lonely I'd been and how much I enjoy having her here, in my home. I relish the comfort her presence brings me. Crave it, in fact, so much so that I agreed to hide the reality that she's alive from her family.

I reach out and pick up the jeans. It's one of five pairs I ordered online yesterday after I realized the effect suits had on Asya. I can't keep walking around in my pajamas all day, and I definitely can't wear them out to the store.

Taking a deep breath, I put on the jeans.

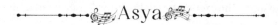

Asya

At least fifteen bags line the counter in a perfect row. Pasha bought way too much stuff.

When he returned from the store an hour ago, he had to go back to the car twice to bring everything up. After he placed the last bag at the end of the long line, he asked me to put away the groceries he brought and to make lunch. Then, he took his laptop and, saying he has some work to do, disappeared into his bedroom.

I unpack the groceries from the first bag, leaving the things I need for lasagna on the kitchen island and storing the rest. I should have been more specific with my grocery list. I assumed he'd get whatever brand of pasta or tomato sauce he comes across first, but instead, he must have purchased every kind available in the store. There are four different brands of lasagna noodles, three tomato sauces, six types of other pasta, and at least ten varieties of cheeses inside the first few bags.

I pull the cereal boxes from the next three bags and count them. There are twelve different kinds: oats, soya, wheat, some with dried fruit or raisins, one is with honey, others include chocolate, and a couple more with almonds.

I glance over my shoulder at the bedroom door. I hoped Pasha would stay in the kitchen or the living room, but he hasn't returned. However, even when he's not in the same room with me, knowing he's here, makes the dreadful voice in my head retreat.

After I'm done putting away the groceries, I look at the last few bags on the counter. They are big boutique bags with wide ribbon handles. Pasha said he would buy something for me to wear. I expected some sweatpants and a few T-shirts, but the bags in front of me are stacked full of clothes. Should I unpack these? He only mentioned the groceries when he asked me to put away the things he bought. I turn around and move to the kitchen island to prepare the lasagna.

Making lunch while only wearing someone else's T-shirt and nothing underneath is weird. Especially in a kitchen belonging to a man I don't really know. Weird, but at the same time liberating. I focus on the task in front of me while a faint melody plays in the back of my mind.

Pavel

"No, you can't bring the buyers to Ural, Sergei," I say into the phone and sigh.

"Why the hell not? Did you look outside? It's fucking freezing. My balls are going to fall off if I take them to the unheated warehouse and have to listen to their rambling for more than ten minutes."

"The last time you conducted a meeting in my club, the cleaning crew spent two hours trying to wash away the blood and brain matter from the VIP booth."

"That was years ago, Pasha!" he barks. "And you changed the upholstery to dark leather last month. Washing the blood off that is a piece of cake."

"I said no."

"*Mudak,*" he mumbles and hangs up.

I shake my head and switch back to the liquor order I've been reviewing on my laptop. Since I won't be heading to the club, I had to take care of the most pressing matters and brief Kostya on the rest. He might be good with numbers, but logistics is not his strong suit. I glance at the time in the corner of the screen and see that it's just after noon. I should check on Asya again.

I've been holed up at the desk in my bedroom for the past three hours, but I've been taking peeks at Asya every fifteen minutes to make sure she's okay. She seemed immersed in cooking lunch, and her relaxed posture said she was enjoying the process. The last time I checked on her, I heard her humming a complicated tune. I expect to find her buzzing around the kitchen this time too, however, she's nowhere in sight.

"Asya?" I call as I hurry across the living room, but there is no answer.

I pass by the dining table, where plates and salad bowls are set for two. A big tray of lasagna, cut into squares, sits between them. I round the kitchen island and come to a halt.

Asya is sitting on the floor with her back pressed to the cupboard, arms wrapped tightly around her legs. She's staring at the window on the far wall with panic in her eyes.

"Asya?" I crouch next to her and place my hand on the back of her neck. "What's wrong?"

"It's . . . snowing," she whispers, eyes locked onto the scene before her.

"You don't like snow?" I ask.

"Not anymore," comes her barely audible answer.

"Asya, give me your eyes, baby." I brush my thumb down her cheek. "Please."

She takes a deep breath, then turns her head. There's such a haunted look in her eyes. Seeing it hits me right in the chest.

"I'm going to pull down the blinds," I say. "Okay?"

"Okay."

Quickly closing the blinds in the kitchen, I head to the living room to pull the heavy curtains over the windows there and rush back. Asya hasn't moved, but now she's staring at the floor.

"I'm sorry," she mumbles and looks up at me with watery eyes.

I crouch in front of her and cup her face between my palms. "You have nothing to be sorry for."

"I'm such a spineless person," she says and presses her lips tightly together.

I lean forward until my face is only inches from hers. "You're reacting because of the reminders. Your mind is being triggered by various things, but it doesn't mean you're weak. Do you understand?"

She sighs and closes her eyes. Something breaks inside me to see her so defeated. I grit my teeth. I need to stay calm for Asya's sake now, but eventually, I'm going to annihilate the sons of bitches who did this to her.

"Mishka. Look at me."

Her eyes open.

"You are not weak," I say. "And you will fight and get better. I promise."

She watches me for a few moments, then leans forward so her mouth is right next to my ear, sliding out of my hold in the process.

"I killed a man," she whispers. "That night, I escaped. I killed my client."

I bite down to hold my rage inside. "Good," I say through gritted teeth.

"I don't regret it. I should. But I don't." Her arm comes around my neck as she presses her cheek to mine. "Does that make me a bad person?"

"No. You defended yourself from a sexual predator who violated you in the most terrible way. In fact, you did him a favor."

"A favor?"

"Yes. Because if you hadn't killed him, I would have. And believe me, whatever you did wouldn't even come close to what I would have done to him." I squeeze the back of her neck lightly. "Come show me what you prepared. It's the first time someone has cooked for me."

Asya leans back, her face right in front of mine again, and places her hand against my cheek. "Thank you. For everything."

CHAPTER
five

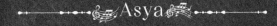
Asya

I PUT ON THE PAJAMAS PASHA BOUGHT FOR ME AND LOOK at myself in the bathroom mirror. The top is not that bad, maybe a size or two too big. The bottoms are a different story. I had to roll the waist and cuff the legs more than twice to make sure they'd stay on and I wouldn't trip while walking. I checked the label and saw that it's size medium. I usually wear extra small.

The rest of the clothes he got lie folded on the long counter next to the sink. All of them are mediums, too. Either Pasha has never shopped for female clothes, or he can't guess sizes that well. I noticed two empty shelves in the cabinet at the other end of the bathroom, so I put the clothes there. I don't want to intrude on his space any more than I already have. I still can't believe he's let me stay.

When I exit the bathroom, Pasha is stepping out of his closet, wearing dark gray pajama bottoms and a black T-shirt.

"I'll leave the door open," he says. "If you need anything, I'll be in the room across the hall."

My body goes rigid upon hearing his words. Wrapping my arms around my middle, I nod and head toward the bed.

"Asya? Is everything okay?"

"Yeah." I climb in bed and turn to face the wall, pulling the blanket all the way up to my chin.

The room falls silent for a moment, but then I hear the sound of bare feet approaching.

"What's wrong?"

I grip the blanket in my hand. "Can you sleep here again?"

"Here? In this bed?"

"Please."

He doesn't say anything. I squeeze my eyes shut, hating myself for asking him. He probably thinks I'm a weakling. As if usurping his life and his space is not enough, I'm asking him to keep sleeping in the same bed with me. I open my mouth to tell him I've changed my mind when the bed dips behind me.

I slide my hands under the pillow, hoping it will stop me from turning toward him and snuggling into his chest. This inexplicable pull I feel toward him confuses me, but it also makes me feel disgusted with myself. I've been assaulted and used in the most degrading ways, so what I should be feeling toward Pasha and any other man is loathing, fear, and repulsion. Instead, I'm attracted to him. But the entire time I've been here, he hasn't once tried anything, hasn't touched me in any way that could be considered sexual.

It's because you're filthy, the voice in my mind whispers. *Spoiled goods no man would ever want to touch. How many dicks have been inside your pussy? Too many to count?*

I turn my face into the pillow. I need it to stop!

You know what you are? A slut. A dirty, filthy whore.

Pasha's thick arm wraps around my waist and pulls me into his body until my back is pressed to his chest.

"Talk to me," he says into my hair.

A shudder passes through my body because of his closeness, and it's not a bad shudder.

"Why didn't you call my brother and get rid of me?" I ask.

"Because I understand the need to deal with your shit yourself. And because I know how it feels to have people get rid of you." The arm around my waist tightens. "I would never do that to anyone."

"You're holed up here with me. Don't you need to go to work?"

"I had someone fill in for me. But I'll have to go for a meeting with the pakhan tomorrow. I won't be long."

My body stiffens as panic rises in the pit of my stomach. It's completely unnatural, the way I have become attached to him, but I can't shake off the feeling of dread that forms from the idea of him not being nearby.

"Okay," I whisper.

"Will you reconsider talking to the psychiatrist?"

I squeeze my lips together and shake my head. Pasha has been trying to convince me to talk with the mental health doctor since this morning. He said she has experience with cases like mine. I can't do it. The thought of talking about it with anyone other than Pasha makes me sick.

"All right, mishka. Let's give it a few more days."

"Does it mean something? Mishka?"

"A bear cub."

He calls me a bear cub. What a strange endearment. I turn my head to look at him. "Is it because I like clinging to you?"

"Yeah." He lifts his hand as if he's going to touch my face, but pulls back. "Let's go to sleep."

I nod and turn back to the wall, pretending I'm trying to sleep. I can't get over the fact that he said yes when I asked him if I can stay instead of sending me back to my family. It was so outrageous, I was a 100 percent sure he'd refuse. He didn't. And I still find it hard to believe that he agreed not to tell anyone who I am.

A light touch grazes the back of my head. I'm not sure what it is, but it seems like a kiss.

CHAPTER
six

─•─•─•─🔫 Pavel 🔫─•─•─•─

"**I**S THAT GIRL STILL AT YOUR PLACE?" ROMAN ASKS as soon as I enter his office.

"Yes." I nod and take a seat next to Maxim.

"Good. You need to ask her how she got the drugs. Yuri still can't locate the guy who supplied the pills, so your girl is our only lead."

I meet my pakhan's gaze and shake my head. "No."

"No?" He widens his eyes at me.

"If she tells me something herself, I'll let you know. But I'm not making her talk unless she wants to."

"Why wouldn't she?"

"Doc hasn't told you?" I ask.

"Told me what? He said you found the girl, she overdosed, and you took her home."

"She was sexually abused, Roman. I think the people who had her were running a prostitution ring."

Roman stares at me, a muscle ticking in his jaw. The pen

in his hands snaps in two. The topic of abused women has always been a sensitive subject where he's concerned.

"Is the girl okay?" he asks through clenched teeth.

"She's better."

"Good. Don't ask her anything." He nods and turns his attention to Maxim. "What's the issue with the Albanians you wanted to discuss?"

Maxim takes off his glasses and crosses his arms over his chest. "It seems like they have suddenly obtained a huge amount of money. One of Anton's guys reported that he saw Dushku's son-in-law spending an insane sum at one of the Cosa Nostra casinos."

"How much?"

"Tens of thousands per night. Several nights in a row."

"Julian is an idiot who never earned a cent himself. He's been milking money off Dushku for years."

"Well, it looks like he suddenly has more than he can spend," Maxim says. "Could he be involved in this new drug thing?"

"He better not be. Because if anyone from the Albanian crime organization dared to bring their drugs into my territory, they won't be liking the consequences of their decision. I made things very clear to Dushku when we had our little chat a few months ago after the fuckup with the Irish."

"What happened with the Irish?" I ask. Since I'm mostly focused on running the clubs, I'm not always up-to-date on other business issues. The latest thing concerning the Irish I remember is that they tried to wipe out the Bratva a few years back and almost killed Kostya. Sergei eliminated their leader and several other top-tier men, and Roman threw the rest out of Chicago.

"They've set up base in New York," Roman says. "Don Ajello sent me a message a few months ago, saying that Dushku started collaborating with the Irish and delivered a large shipment of guns to them. Dushku did this despite knowing very well my stance on the Irish."

"Was it only one shipment?" I ask. "Or does Dushku still work with them?"

"Just one. Shortly after that, Ajello took care of the Irish because the idiot Fitzgerald kidnapped his wife. Ajello went ballistic."

"He killed Fitzgerald?"

"Filleted him with a knife himself." Roman grins. "I don't know the man, but I like him already."

"What do you plan on doing with the Albanians, Roman?" Maxim throws in.

"Do we have anyone inside who can keep an eye on what they are doing? We need to know where that money came from."

"One of the Baykal waitresses visits Dushku regularly," I say. "Maybe she can persuade him to talk about his business."

"Let's try that for now." He nods. "If it does end up that Dushku is behind this, I'm going to personally gut him."

As I exit my car, heading to the front of my apartment building, I notice a familiar vehicle parked outside the entrance. Yuri is sitting behind the wheel of his white SUV, waving me over.

"What's going on?" I ask as I slide onto the passenger seat.

He leans his elbows on the steering wheel and pins me with his gaze. "I don't know. You tell me."

"Nothing. Why?"

He shakes his head and looks toward the street beyond the windshield. "I've known you for ten years, Pasha, so don't give me this shit. Are you planning to leave the Bratva?"

"No. Why would you think that?"

"You let Kostya take over your clubs. You've practically lived at Ural and wouldn't let anyone cover for you, ever. When I tried convincing you to take a break a few months back, you said you can't function unless you're working."

"Well, I've decided to take that break now."

"So, you're coming back?"

I slouch back in the seat and look up at my building. It's been about three hours since I left for the meeting with Roman, and I've spent every single second of that time thinking about Asya. Is she okay? Has she eaten? What if she's hungry and can't decide what to make? Is she scared having been left alone? What if I come home and she won't be there?

"I'll come back, Yuri. Don't worry."

"When?"

"When she leaves," I say, looking up toward the windows on the third floor. I can't see the lights inside because the blinds are closed. What if she got scared again? I hate leaving her alone.

"She? The girl you have at your place?"

"Yes."

"Are you two . . . in a relationship?"

"No."

"I don't understand."

I glance at my friend. His jaw is clenched tight and there

is a concern in his eyes. At sixty-five, Yuri is the oldest in the Bratva's inner circle. He has become a father figure to the soldiers who work under him, but he's also fiercely protective of the rest of the Bratva's men, regardless of their position. I've always found it strange, how he can care so greatly about the guys who aren't his family, while there are people in the world who don't give a fuck about their own flesh and blood.

"Have you ever met someone who feels like they are a missing piece of you?" I ask. "A piece you didn't even know you were missing until they stumbled into your life?"

"No, not really. You think that girl is yours?"

"I've known her for a week."

"That's not what I asked."

"I know. But it doesn't really matter. She'll be leaving soon, anyway." I grab the door handle. "I'm coming back to work as soon as she does."

"Maybe she won't want to leave."

"Yeah, sure," I say and exit the car.

CHAPTER
seven

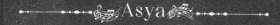
Asya

I AM STANDING IN THE MIDDLE OF THE SHOWER STALL, staring at the two bottles on the corner shelf. The black one is the bodywash for men I've been using since I got here. It has a woodsy scent with a hint of citrus and sage. It was there from the start, and it was the only one. Now, there is a different shower gel next to it. A pink bottle with flowers on it. Pasha must have brought and left it here for me. I take a deep breath and reach for it, but the instant my fingers come close to the bottle, anxiety rises within my chest. I look back at the black bottle and move my hand to it. The anxiety intensifies. I let my hand fall. I spend more than fifteen minutes watching the stupid soap bottles and gritting my teeth to the point of my jaw hurting. I finally grab both and send them flying across the bathroom, where they hit the wall and fall to the floor.

A bang sounds on the door. "Asya!"

I lean my back against the tiled wall as my breath comes in shallow bursts. This is the first time I've tried to take a shower without Pasha being in the bathroom with me. I felt so proud of myself earlier when I told him he didn't have to come in with me. He smiled a little and said he would stay on the other side of the door just in case.

"Asya?" Another bang. "I'm coming in!"

The door bursts open and Pasha rushes in, looking around himself. His eyes fall to the bottles on the floor, and then his gaze snaps to me. His metallic gray depths, not light blue as I originally thought, scan me from head to toe—questioning, assessing...worried. Their intensity draws me in, grounding me in a way that eases my anxiety.

"I couldn't choose which fucking bodywash to use," I say and close my eyes, feeling completely defeated.

"Shit," Pasha mumbles. A few seconds later, his rough palm caresses my cheek. "I'm sorry. I wasn't thinking."

"It's not your fault I'm a basket case." I sigh.

"You're not a basket case, mishka."

"Yeah, sure." I snort. "You should take me to the nearest mental hospital and leave me there."

"Asya, look at me."

I open my eyes to find him standing in front of me, his hand still on my cheek, and the other on the wall next to my head.

"It will get better," he says. "I promise."

"You don't know that."

"I do. You're a fighter. It'll take time, but you will get better. Come on, let's get you washed up. Okay?"

I nod reluctantly.

"Good. I'll go get that shower gel."

I watch him walk toward the other end of the bathroom and pick the bottles off the floor. Then, he returns inside the shower stall.

"This one is mine," he says as he places the black one back onto the shelf, "and the pink one is yours. You'll use that one."

How can he be so calm? It's as if my throwing a fit doesn't bother him in the least.

"Now, what else is the problem?" He looks down at me.

I bite my lower lip. "The towels."

"The towels?"

"Bath towels. You have blue and white ones." I keep using the hand towels after my shower because those are all white.

"I'll use blue. You have the white. Does that work?"

I nod, feeling like a complete idiot. Pasha's fingers lightly grip my chin, tilting my head up. "Any other problems with the bathroom?"

"No," I whisper.

"Okay. Should I wait here?"

I don't want him to leave, but I shake my head anyway. It's not easy, but after his instructions, I can handle the shower alone because I know he will still be close by.

He smiles. "Shower. Dress. I'll be waiting outside, and we'll have breakfast when you're done."

Pasha's thumb brushes lightly along my jaw before his hand falls away from my face. He turns and leaves the bathroom. Slowly, I raise my hand and retrace the path of his touch.

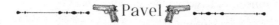

Pavel

I place a cereal box on the counter in front of Asya and head toward the fridge to get the milk. When I put the carton next to the cereal, she reaches for it, but I take her hand in mine.

"Not yet," I say.

With my free hand, I open the cupboard and take out a jar of marmalade. I place it next to the cereal box, grab the peanut butter and bread, and line everything up on the counter. Asya tilts her head to the side, watching me.

I move to stand behind her and nod toward the things on the counter. "What would you like to have for breakfast?"

Asya looks over the assortment of food and flattens her lips.

She's been here for two weeks. Every morning I've given her milk and selected a cereal, making sure it was a different flavor each time. Asya always made us both a bowl, and we had breakfast in the dining room. It distresses her when she needs to make even the most trivial decision, so I've tried my best to make it easier on her. But it's time she pushes beyond her comfort zone, even a tiny bit.

"Why are you doing this?" she asks through her teeth.

"What?"

"Asking me to choose."

"If you can't, I'll help you." I reach to place my hand on her waist, but I catch myself and press my palm onto the cold counter instead. "But maybe you can try. It's just food. You can't make a wrong choice, so don't worry."

She grabs the edge of the counter in front of her and stares at the items. A minute passes. Then five more.

"It's okay," I say. "Take your time."

The need to stroke her back or place a kiss in her hair is eating me alive. I forgot myself once and kissed her on the back of the head. Hopefully, she was already asleep and didn't notice it. She would probably feel revolted if she finds out I'm attracted to her. It's wrong on so many levels. When she mentioned the other day that she's only eighteen, it only made the situation worse. She is fifteen years younger than me. I need to keep my distance as much as possible.

"I can't." Asya's nails scrape the top of the counter as she tightens her grip, her gaze fixed on the cereal box.

"Of course you can," I say as I battle the need to touch her.

It guts me each time I see her struggling to make even the most basic choice. She still doesn't want to talk with the psychologist, so I've been calling every two days to ask for guidance. The psychologist recommended I create a situation where Asya would need to make a small decision, but I'm not supposed to insist if it makes her too uncomfortable. The doctor tells me every time that for Asya to get better, she needs professional help. However, it can only happen if Asya is ready to accept it.

A few seconds later, I see Asya's right hand creeping forward, toward the cereal, then it stops. I move the box closer but make sure it's still far enough that she needs to reach for it.

"You said you liked to eat cereal at home," I say. "Do you think your preferences have changed?"

"No."

"Then it's safe to say that you'd pick cereal. Come on, just a few more inches."

Asya purses her lips together and, the next moment, her hand closes the distance to the box. She grabs it and presses it into her chest as if it's something utterly precious.

"I did it," she mumbles.

"See? It'll get better."

She spins and wraps her free hand around my wrist while her gaze bores into mine. Her palm moves upward, along my forearm.

"Thank you," she says and leans into me slightly.

"Any time, mishka." I reluctantly take a step back. "Let's eat. I'm starving."

A strange expression crosses Asya's face as her hand falls from my arm. She turns away and busies herself with pouring the milk and cereal into matching black bowls. I don't think I ever used these before she came. In fact, more than half of the kitchen wares were unused, tidily stored away in drawers and cupboards. Of all the stuff I own, I've only used two plates, some glasses, and a few coffee cups. I'm not certain, but I may have used the stove only a time or two.

When Asya is done pouring the cereal, I carry the bowls to the dining room. She follows a step behind me, clutching the hem of my shirt in her hand, something she still does most of the time. Only after I reach the table does she let go of my tee and take the chair on my right.

She is so quiet all the time. When she eats. When she walks around my place. Even when she cooks. There is no clanging of pots or silverware, no noise whatsoever unless she's humming to herself. I can't decipher the song, but the melody sounds familiar.

I wonder if she was so quiet before, or if it's a consequence of everything that's happened to her. But there's still fire left in her. It might be suppressed deep inside, but it's there. Whoever hurt her, didn't extinguish it completely.

CHAPTER eight

"**R**EADY?" I ASK.

Asya is standing in the middle of the bedroom with her arms wrapped around her midsection. "No."

"We need to get you some clothes. Nothing I bought fits." I nod toward the shirt she's wearing which is at least two sizes too big. The legs of the blue jeans she's got on are rolled up, as well. How did I fuck this up so much? When I was buying the clothes, they seemed small to me. Asya might only stay with me for a short time, but I won't let her go around pulling the sleeves of her shirts nonstop. I want her to feel comfortable. "The store is close by and we'll be the only ones there."

Asya looks down at the floor, biting her lower lip.

"Asya. Look at me, baby," I say, and she reluctantly lifts her head. "I won't let go of your hand, no matter what. You will be safe."

"You said 'safe,'" she mumbles. "You didn't say 'it's going to be okay.' Why?"

"Because it probably won't be okay. You may get scared because it's the first time you're going out in public after almost three weeks. You may even freak out." I squeeze her hand. "But you will be safe the whole time. Do you understand what I'm saying, mishka?"

Asya's eyes find mine and, for a moment, I'm taken aback by the trust I see in their depths. Roman trusted me with his clubs when he assigned me to manage them. But no one has trusted their life to me before. Feeling safe is one of the most basic human needs, and she just placed her faith in me.

"Do you want to take the car or walk there?" I ask. "It's just two blocks away."

She just watches me, her lips pressed tight. Looks like she's still having trouble making decisions herself, but she is getting better. This morning she opened the fridge and took out the milk to make cereal for breakfast, she probably did it without thinking about it. Before today, she would just open the fridge and stare inside until I came and picked up the milk for her. I would never admit it, because it's absolutely selfish, but I secretly enjoy it.

I have never needed anyone, or better said, I've never let myself need anyone. And no one has ever needed me. That concept was completely foreign to me until now. The idea of Asya needing me feeds a yearning that I couldn't name before.

We're still sharing my bed. For the first couple of nights, I thought about using one of the other bedrooms, but I'd see the fear in her eyes when I tried to leave and go back to lie next to her instead. At some point, I stopped trying. I love how she snuggles into me when she awakes from a nightmare, as if being close to me is enough to chase away the monsters.

81

"We'll head out on foot, then," I say and leave the room with her following, her hand tightly clasped in mine.

We are the only customers in the small boutique I picked. I called the owner earlier and instructed him to make sure no one else is let inside until we're done. I also requested to have the store cleared of all personnel except the one attendant at the cash register, who was also told not to leave her spot.

Asya comes to a stop in the middle of the store and looks around, her eyes skimming along the long racks of clothes and the shelves of shoes. She takes everything in, inhaling a deep breath, and squeezes my hand.

"Let's start with underwear," I say and lead her to the far corner of the store.

Asya peruses the things on display but doesn't make a move to pick anything up. Her eyes wander over the underwear, lingering on some items for a few seconds longer than others. It's usually the bright colors that draw her attention. She passes over the white pieces as if they're not even there.

I pay attention to her gaze as she looks at the displayed undergarments, noting every article her eyes land on for a split-second longer than the rest. After she's done with the displays, I pick up the smallest size of every item that caught her attention.

"All good?" I look down at her and find her watching me. Her eyes are brimming with unshed tears. I brush her cheek with the back of my hand, then nod toward the rack on my left. "Let's do shirts next."

We repeat the ordeal in every section of the store, and since my hands end up filled with clothes, Asya switches to holding the sleeve of my jacket. When we reach the changing room, I enter the stall and place the heap of clothes, along with the yellow coat she ogled for almost a minute and two pairs of shoes, onto the bench by the mirror.

"You can let go of my jacket and try on everything," I say. She nods but doesn't let it go.

I reach for the first shirt on the pile and offer it to her. "You're safe, mishka. No one can hurt you while I'm here."

The corners of Asya's lips lift a little, and she slowly releases her hold.

It takes her more than half an hour to try on everything, and only a few items end up being too big. I collect the clothes that fit under one arm and, taking her hand in mine, we leave the changing room. As I'm paying at the cash register, the chime of the bells over the door rings out behind us. I turn around just in time to see an older man in a gray suit coming inside the store.

"Mr. Morozov!" he smiles, walking toward us. "I hope your shopping experience went as requested?"

Asya stiffens, her hand squeezing mine in a mad grip. I look down at her to find her staring at the boutique manager with horror in her eyes.

"Come, baby," I say, sliding my arm around her middle. She jumps up and tightly wraps her arms and legs in a familiar pose.

"Was everything to your liking?" the idiot keeps rambling as he approaches us. "I specifically—"

I grab the store manager by the collar of his dress shirt with my free hand while supporting Asya with the other. I jerk him around and slam him against the concrete pillar next to the cash register.

"What the fuck did I tell you?" I bark into his face.

"I . . . I . . . please!"

"I said only one person, a female, is allowed in here until we leave." I shove him into the pillar again, then one more time for good measure. "Are you a fucking female?"

"No . . . please . . ."

"No. You are not!" I snap.

Fingers are in my hair, passing through the strands. Once. Twice. I turn my head to the side slightly and my cheek presses to Asya's.

"He meant no harm," she whispers next to my ear.

"The road to hell is paved with good intentions," I say. "Do you know that quote?"

"Yes." Another stroke through my hair. "It's both true and idiotic. Let the man go."

"No one scares you and gets away without punishment." I release my hold on the store manager's shirt and backhand him before turning to the counter to collect our bags.

I leave the store with Asya in my arms and carry her the two blocks to my building. A few people we pass throw dumbfounded looks in our direction, but they quickly look away when they see the angry scowl on my face. Most of Asya's tension eased shortly after we left the boutique, but she keeps her face snuggled in the crook of my neck, her arms and legs clutching to me with all her strength. Stupid motherfucker, I should have just snapped his neck for scaring her. I'm still so fucking livid, I have to resist the urge to turn around and do that exact thing.

When we reach my building, I don't even nod to the

security guy in the lobby, just head right into the elevator and hit the button for the third floor with my elbow. As soon as we're inside my place, I let the bags fall to the floor and walk to the living room. Asya is still plastered to my body as I sit down on the sofa.

"You can let go, mishka," I say and stroke my palm down her hair.

She just shakes her head and presses her face more into my neck. A soft sigh escapes her, and then I feel something wet on my skin.

"Please don't be sad, baby."

Asya takes a deep breath and leans away, looking at me. Tears are falling down her cheeks, and her eyes are red and puffy. But she doesn't look sad. She looks mad as hell.

"I'm so sick of this," she says through her teeth and grabs at the front of my jacket. "So. Fucking. Sick."

"I know."

Her hands let go of my jacket and she takes my face between her palms, staring into my eyes. "I want to go to the mall."

Our gazes are locked. It feels like I could drown in the dark depths of her eyes, it makes it hard to think straight. "I don't think that's a good idea, Asya."

"I can't live like this. Panicking because of the most basic things. Hiding here, in your place." Her hands move to the back of my head, threading the strands between her fingers. "I want my life back. I want myself back."

Her last sentence is barely audible. I lift my hand and brush the tears from her cheeks with my thumb. "Okay."

Asya nods and her eyes fall to my lips. Her hands are still raking my hair. As I watch, she takes a deep breath and leans forward. She's going to kiss me. God, I've been thinking about kissing her for days, hating myself for having the idea festering in my mind. She is too young, and she's been terribly hurt. Letting her kiss me would be no better than making a move on a traumatized girl.

"Asya," I whisper. "Please don't, baby."

Asya

My body goes rigid upon hearing Pasha's words. I look up to find his eyes regarding me with concern. Just a couple of inches are separating my mouth from his. If I'm quick, I might be able to steal one quick kiss, even if he doesn't want it.

But as fast as that thought enters my mind, another follows. No, I know what's it like to have something taken from you against your will. I can't do it to him.

"Why not?" I ask. "You don't want spoiled goods, is that the issue?"

Pasha's eyes widen and the next instant his hand shoots up, grabbing my chin. "Don't you ever say that again," he says through his teeth. "Ever."

"Then why, Pasha? Is it bad that I want to kiss you?" I lean into his hand, intending to close the distance between us, but he doesn't allow me to.

He doesn't say anything, just stares at me, his nostrils flaring. I wonder if he's aware that while he's holding me away from him with his left hand, his right is still stroking my cheek. I sigh and straighten, letting go of his hair.

The phone in his pocket rings. He reaches for it and

presses it to his ear, listening to what the person on the other side is saying. I can hear the faint voice from the other end. It's male and sounds agitated, but I can't understand what is being said because he's speaking Russian.

"I'll come over," Pasha replies in English, then lowers the phone.

"You need to go to work?"

"Yes. I'm in charge of the Bratva's club business. I'll be back in a couple of hours," he says. "Will you be okay?"

I don't want him to go, but I nod anyway.

"I've ordered some groceries; they will leave them at the front door. If you're tired of cooking, I'll order something for you from the restaurant across the street." He brushes the side of my chin with the tip of his finger. "But if you want to make something for dinner and can't decide what, there is a laptop on the nightstand in the bedroom. Google quick dishes and pick the first one you know how to make. Okay?"

I nod again. He doesn't release my chin. Instead, his fingers move along my jaw to the back of my neck where he buries them in my hair.

"I emptied the dresser in the bedroom, you can put your new clothes there."

So, he noticed that I freaked out when I saw the suits in his closet. "Do you really need to leave?"

"I won't be long." He looks over at the clock on the wall. "I need to go over some paperwork with Kostya before the club opens at ten. I'll be back by ten thirty."

"Can you take the clock down?"

Pasha looks down at me, and I can see the question in his eyes.

"I'm nearsighted," I say.

His hand on my nape moves back to my chin and tilts my head up. "Why haven't you told me?"

I shrug.

"Do you wear glasses or contacts?"

"Glasses. Contacts irritate my eyes."

His other hand cups my face and he glides his palm up, brushing his thumbs along my eyebrows and then over the sensitive skin under my eyes. "We'll get you glasses tomorrow when we go to the mall."

He lets go of my face and removes his wristwatch. "Would this work?" he asks.

I stare at the expensive gold watch he placed in my hand. It's still warm from touching his skin. "Yeah," I choke out.

"Okay." He nods. "Take a shower. You have three pairs of pajamas—they're all the same so you don't have to choose. Put away your new clothes. Eat. Wait for me. In bed, not on the floor in front of the door."

I get down off his lap and watch him leave, then head into the bathroom to have a shower.

I grip the wristwatch in my hand. Half past eleven. I've been sitting in bed for two and a half hours, staring at this thing, and with each passing minute, the panic in the pit of my stomach intensifies.

I did everything Pasha told me to do within the hour, including preparing risotto with chicken. It was the first dish that showed up in my Google search. Making food was usually my task at home. I quite enjoy cooking, so I can prepare almost anything except seafood. The slippery feel of it in my hands always made me cringe, so Arturo was in charge of that. My brother is an amazing cook, and he's the one who taught me everything. He tried to coax Sienna into learning, too, but my sister burned everything. My guess is she couldn't cook and simultaneously post dozens of photos on social media.

I look down at the watch again. Twenty to midnight. Where is he?

CHAPTER
nine

●───·•───── ◄ Pavel ► ─────•·───●

Three hours earlier

EVERYBODY IS STARING. THE TWO SECURITY GUARDS
at the back entrance of the club. The cleaning lady
mopping around the tables. The barman. I ignore
them and climb the narrow stairs leading to the gallery
housing our administrative spaces that overlook the dance
floor.

I pass the room where two security guys are hunched in
front of the screens, watching the camera feeds, and enter my
office. Kostya is sitting behind my desk, looking at the monitor and clicking angrily on the mouse. The whole tabletop
is covered with papers. Off to the side, there are two empty
coffee cups and a half-eaten sandwich with crumbs scattered
everywhere.

"Such a pig." I shake my head.

"You picked the worst fucking time to take a vacation,"
he mumbles and keeps hitting the mouse. "The contracts with

liquor suppliers need to be renewed. Two waitresses are sick and another is going on maternity leave. The surveillance system crashed twice yesterday. I forgot to order . . ." He looks up and scans me from head to toe. "Who the fuck are you and what have you done with Pavel?"

I nod toward the mess on the desk. "Clean this shit up so I can sit down and see what else you've fucked up."

"Jeans? Really? And a fucking hoodie?" he raises his eyebrows, then bursts out laughing. "Pasha, sweetheart, are you all right?"

"Hilarious. Get up."

"Yuri called," he says and collects the cups. "They found the guy who supplied those pills. He's bringing him here."

"Good." I sit down and sort through the contracts strewn across the desk. Some have round brown stains on them. "Wait for them downstairs and take the guy to the back room when they arrive."

"Okay. Are you sure you don't want me to call the doc to check your head?"

"Fuck off, Kostya."

I'm almost done with the mess Kostya made when gunfire explodes downstairs. Grabbing my weapon from the drawer, I rush into the surveillance room.

"What's happening?" I yell.

"Yuri and two soldiers came in two minutes ago, dragging some guy with them. Those vehicles arrived after them," the security guy says and points to the screen showing the back alley. Two cars with tinted windows are parked just around the corner. "Eight people came out, killed the guards, and came inside the club."

"Call Dimitri. Tell him we need backup and Doc. Then,

get downstairs. Now!" I rush toward the door while gunshots keep ringing out below.

The dance floor is covered in blood. Three hostiles are down in the center, and two feet away, the body of a waiter is sprawled with his face to the ground. Across the room, there are two more bodies, probably the soldiers who arrived with Yuri. Kostya is crouched behind the bar, shooting at two men near the entrance. I aim at the first one and shoot him in the head. The other one turns in my direction but falls when Kostya's bullet strikes his neck.

"The rest?" I shout as I'm running down the stairs.

"They went in the back." Kostya jumps over the bar and rushes toward the hallway leading to the storage area. "Yuri is alone in there!"

I don't hear any gunfire as I run after Kostya. That's not good. He turns left and I follow just a few paces behind. We barge into the back room at the same time, our weapons raised.

One hostile is facedown on the floor near the metal cabinet that stores the cleaning supplies. On the right, there are two more men. One is obviously dead, a hole in his forehead. There is a big red splatter on the wall above him. The one next to him is still alive, but he's been shot in the thigh and shoulder. I walk toward him and collect his gun and his comrade's. Another man in cargo pants and a checkered shirt is sprawled on the middle of the floor, several gunshot wounds are in his back. His hands are tied. It's probably the guy who supplied the drugs.

"Yuri!" Kostya yells somewhere behind me. I turn and a chill flushes over me.

Yuri is sitting on the floor with his back on the wall. His

whole torso is covered in blood. I rush to kneel next to Kostya, who rips off his shirt and presses it over the wound in Yuri's stomach. I take off my hoodie, too, bundle it up and shove it against the other wound in the middle of Yuri's chest. Kostya's white shirt over Yuri's stomach is already saturated, and blood is seeping through his fingers.

"Where the fuck is the doc!" I bark and grab Yuri by the back of his neck. "Yuri! Open your eyes!"

His eyes slowly flutter open, but the look in them is unfocused.

"Stay with us! Yuri! The doc is coming," I shout.

He tries to tell me something, but it's too faint.

"Don't." I squeeze his neck. "We'll speak when the doc patches you up."

Next to me, Kostya takes out his phone and dials. Dear God, there is so much blood. I carefully run my hands over Yuri's chest and sides and find another wound above his hip.

"Fuck." I frantically take off my T-shirt, pressing it over the injury. "Yuri, no. Don't close your eyes. Stay with us."

He takes a shallow breath and lifts his hand to grab my upper arm, pulling me toward him.

"Albanians," he says next to my ear, then coughs. "I heard them . . . speaking to each other."

The hold on my arm loosens, and Yuri's hand falls to the floor. His dark blue eyes are still on me, but they look glassy. Two rivulets of blood are trailing down from the corners of his mouth.

"Yuri!" I yell into his face. "Don't you dare die on me! Yuri!"

"Pasha," Kostya says. "He's gone."

No! Yuri is responsible for giving me the only family I've ever known—the Bratva. He can't be gone.

"Yuri!" I shake him.

"Pavel, stop," A rough voice says behind me, and I look up to find the doc standing there.

"You're late!" I yell.

"There is nothing anyone could have done," Doc says, nodding to the floor. "He lost too much blood."

I slowly lay Yuri down, stand up, and head toward the opposite end of the room. Grabbing the only living Albanian by his neck, I punch him in the face with all my strength.

"Why?" I ask, then punch him again. "Why were you here?"

"To dispose . . . of Davis," he mumbles.

I punch his head again. And again.

"Pasha! That's enough!"

I ignore Kostya's yelling and continue hitting the motherfucker while the smell of blood invades my nostrils. Someone tries to shove me away, but I shake them off and keep plowing my fists into the Albanian's face until all that is left of it is a mass of blood and red flesh.

When I'm done, I let the body fall to the floor and head toward one of the cabinets. I take out two white linen tablecloths and carry them to where the doc is kneeling next to Yuri's body. I use one to wipe the blood off my friend's face, then close his eyes and carefully cover him with the clean linen.

"Prashchay, bratan," I say, then turn and head toward the door, passing Kostya along the way.

"Jesus fuck," Kostya mumbles, staring at the body of the man I killed with my bare hands. "I'm gonna puke."

When I get back into my office, I grab a vodka from the minibar and take a hefty drag directly from the bottle. It tastes even more awful than I remember. Sitting down in the recliner by the minibar, I take another pull. I don't recall the last time I got drunk.

Someone yells downstairs. Looks like Roman's arrived. I lift the bottle and drink again. Five minutes later, more noise—something's breaking. It sounds like someone is throwing around pieces of furniture. More shouting.

"Dimitri!" Roman roars "Get Angelina on the phone. Fucking now!"

Sounds like Sergei is here, as well. I stand up, bottle in hand, and walk toward the glass wall to look at the scene below. Sergei is standing in the middle of the dance floor, gripping a broken bar stool in his hand. Roman is facing him, his palm is extended toward his brother, and he's saying something to Sergei, who looks like he's going to smash the stool over Roman's head at any second. Dimitri approaches them from the side, holding a phone in his outstretched hand. Sergei's head snaps toward the phone, his gaze zeroing in on the device. The stool crashes to the floor. Sergei grabs the phone out of Dimitri's hand, presses it to his ear, and listens for a few moments. He then throws the phone back to Dimitri and leaves.

I should probably stay and see if they need my help, but I can't stomach the idea. Yuri is gone. The look in his eyes as he stared at me during those last few seconds of his life is going to haunt me for the rest of mine. I shake my head and set off toward the fire escape.

I find Kostya leaning on the wall near the back exit. He looks over at me, then at the bottle in my hand.

"Since when do you drink alcohol?" he asks.

"Since today." I tip my head toward his car. "I need a ride."

We don't speak during the half-hour drive to my place, both of our gazes fixed on the street in front of us. It's started snowing again, and I find myself fixated on the white flakes falling from the sky. I guess I don't like snow anymore, either.

I close my eyes, lean back in the seat, and take another heavy gulp from the bottle.

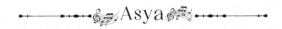

Asya

The front door bangs open, and I exhale with relief. He's back. A moment later something crashes to the floor.

"Pasha?" I shout.

There are a couple of seconds of silence before I hear his voice.

"It's me, mishka." His voice is strange. Strangled.

I expect him to come into the bedroom, but he doesn't. I stare at the open door. Then, there's a sound of glass breaking and a thud.

"Pasha?"

Nothing. I tense. Something's happened. I throw the blanket off, intending to go look for him, but I can't make myself move. He said to wait for him in bed. Should I stay here? Or go and see what happened? I can't decide.

"Pasha?" I call again. No reply.

My hands start shaking. Something bad has happened. I know it because this is so unlike him. I move toward the edge of the bed, and the tremors in my hands intensify while nausea claws its way up my throat. The thought of leaving the bed makes me want to weep. Grabbing a handful of the bed-sheets in my fingers, I squeeze and try to swallow down the bile. Finally, I dash across the bedroom at breakneck speed, hitting my elbow on the doorway. I misjudged the distance. Ignoring the pain, I burst into the living room.

"Pasha?"

The lamp in the corner is on, illuminating the room in a dim, dusk-like glow. The front door is hanging wide open. The narrow table near the door where Pasha leaves his keys lies overturned on the floor. He's nowhere in sight.

I head toward the overturned console and feel something wet and sticky on the floor under my bare feet. I know the light switch is close, so I start feeling the wall with my palm. My sight is worse when there's not enough light. Both the switch and the wall are white, making it hard to spot. When I find it, I turn on the lights and look around.

Pasha is sitting on the floor in the kitchen, leaning with his back against the oven door. His eyes are closed. There are pieces of glass everywhere, and the smell of alcohol is in the air.

"Pasha?"

He opens his eyes and cocks his head to the side, regarding me. "I'm sorry I'm late."

Careful not to step on the glass, I cross the kitchen and crouch between his legs. He doesn't look like himself. His hair is a mess, and he's wearing only jeans. His bare chest is splattered with what looks like dried blood. And I'm pretty sure he's drunk. I reach out and cup his face in my palms.

"What happened?" I ask.

He closes his eyes and leans forward until his forehead touches mine.

"Someone died, mishka," he whispers.

I move my hands through his dark blond hair. One of the strands keeps falling forward, across his eye.

"Who?" I try moving that tress of hair off, but it ends up over his face again.

"Yuri. One of the Bratva's enforcers. A friend."

"What happened?"

"Three weeks ago, we caught a guy dealing drugs—pills—at our club. It was the same substance that was used on you. Yuri found the man who supplied the pills and brought him to the club to be questioned."

"Did you get some answers?"

"No. A group of men followed them and charged inside, shooting. They killed five of our men, then went to the back where Yuri was with the prisoner." He shakes his head. "Killed them both."

"I'm so sorry," I whisper and lean forward, placing a kiss at the center of his forehead. "So very sorry."

He looks at me then, our eyes so close, and as I stare into his, my heart flutters. It feels like a butterfly is trapped within my chest. I want to kiss him or comfort him in any way I can. The way he did for me. But I don't know if he'll welcome it. So instead, I just brush the back of my fingers down his cheek.

"Let's go to bed, Pasha."

He takes a deep breath and slowly rises, pulling me up with him. When we're both standing, he looks at the kitchen floor covered in glass shards.

"Shit. Please tell me you didn't cut yourself."

"I'm fine. Let's go."

Pasha's gaze falls to my bare feet. "Step on top of my toes."

"Why?"

"I don't think it's wise to carry you while I'm in this state, mishka."

I'm about to say I can get back by myself but change my mind. Wrapping my arms around Pasha's waist, I place my right foot over his shoe, then the left. His left hand slides to my back, pressing me closer to his body.

"We'll go slow," he says. "Hold tight."

"Okay," I murmur and press my cheek to his chest. I'll probably end up with blood on my face, but I don't care.

Pasha grabs the side of the counter with his free hand and takes a step forward. Then one more. I keep myself pressed to his body as he walks through the kitchen. The glass shards break under the soles of his shoes with each step. When we reach the living room, he braces his palm on the wall and looks down at me. There is no glass this far from the kitchen, but I don't remove my feet from the top of his. Instead, I squeeze his waist tighter. Something passes between us, like an exchange without words being spoken. He's silently telling me I'm safe to let him go, but I answer that I won't, even if there is no need to hold him anymore. As if acknowledging my unspoken reply, Pasha nods and resumes walking us all the way to the bedroom.

When we reach the bed, I release his waist and climb under the covers. Holding up the corner of the duvet, I pat the pillow next to my head. Pasha watches me for a few moments, then removes his shoes and slips under the covers next to me.

"Tell me about your friend," I say and snuggle into his side. "What was he like?"

"I met Yuri ten years ago. He came to one of my fights.

After the match was over, he approached me and asked if I'd like to focus my energy and skills somewhere else."

"Fights?" I ask.

The silent pause lasts almost a minute. "Before I joined the Bratva, I earned money by fighting in underground matches," he finally says. I can't see his face, but his voice is clipped. Is he worried that I might think less of him because of how he earned his living?

I press my hand on the center of his chest and bury my face into his neck. "Yuri recruited you for the Bratva?"

"Yes. He was in charge of foot soldiers. Three years later, when the guy who ran the clubs was killed, the pakhan promoted me to the position, saying that my three-piece suits made the other soldiers fidgety. But Yuri was always around, pestering me to go out with the guys. He said I needed to loosen up."

"And did you? Follow his advice?"

"Nope. I'm not really a people person, mishka."

Yeah. I got that impression, too. I move my hand up and thread my fingers through the hair at the back of his head. A melody comes to mind. "The Rain Must Fall" by Yanni. Slow and sad. Peaceful. I hum the tune as I pass my fingers through Pasha's hair.

"Why did you let me stay here?" I ask.

Pasha sighs and places his chin on the top of my head. "I don't know. Why did you want to stay?"

I've been asking myself that question for weeks. "I don't know, either."

CHAPTER Ten

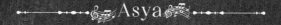

Asya

THE ELEVATOR DOOR LOOMS IN FRONT OF ME, AND I desperately try to control the panic building within. I'm failing miserably.

"Don't let go of my hand," I whisper as bile creeps up my throat.

"I won't," Pasha says next to me.

There is a ding, signaling that we've reached the mall's ground floor. The doors open. The moment I glimpse people milling around, I take a quick step back. Pasha's hand shoots out to the side, hitting the button to close the door.

"You can do this, mishka," he says. "But if you're not ready, we'll try again next week."

No, I'm not ready. I don't think I'll ever be ready. But I'm doing it anyway. And I'm doing it today.

"Open the door, please," I choke out and squeeze Pasha's hand.

The first minute is the worst. It's early, so the mall is not crowded at all, but still, it feels like I'm going to suffocate just by being here. The sight of people in such an enclosed space, the sounds they make, their looks—everything seems too much. Pasha squeezes my hand back and takes a step forward.

Someone is laughing. They are farther away, down the hallway, but it seems like they are right next to me. The sound of feet thumping on the floor and random chatter echo in my ears. I shut my eyes and hold my breath. There is a light touch on my face, the tip of Pasha's finger trailing the line of my jaw. I take another breath and open my eyes. He's standing in front of me, blocking the view of the crowd with his wide frame.

"It's okay, baby," he says. "No one can hurt you when I'm here. Just look into my eyes."

He moves his hand to the back of my neck and takes a step backward, pulling me with him. Without letting go of his gaze, I step forward. His lips curve upward. He takes another step, and then one more. I follow. I can still hear the people, but the sounds don't bother me that much anymore because all my focus is centered on the man in front of me.

I don't think anyone would call Pasha beautiful. The lines on his face are too harsh. His right eyebrow is split in two by a thin scar. His nose is too big and slightly crooked. He doesn't look like a man you'd want to ask on a date, but rather someone you'd want to have by your side when walking in a dark alley. Though, if someone asked me how a perfect man should look, I would point to the one standing before me.

Two more steps. I match his pace. Out of the corner of my eye, I see people looking in our direction with wonder on their faces. Several more steps, and Pasha stops.

"We're here." Pasha nods toward the store on his right.

I throw a quick look to the side. It's the optical retailer.

"Do you want to go inside now, or would you prefer we come back later?" he asks.

"Now." I nod and take another step toward him, molding my front to his.

His hand slides from my neck to my hair, and I can feel the heat of his body seeping into mine. I want more, need more of it. I lift my palm and place it on the center of his chest. People are passing us by, some grumbling that we're in the way, but neither of us moves. Pasha's head dips slightly, and I hold my breath, wondering if he's going to kiss me. He doesn't. Instead, he releases my hair and takes a step away.

"Let's go find some glasses for you," he says and heads inside the shop.

I'm standing next to Pasha as he gives the store attendant his address so they can deliver my new glasses once they're ready when a man enters the store and heads toward the rack of sunglasses. He's holding a phone to his ear, talking to someone. My eyes skim his dress pants and white shirt and stop on his bright red tie. I should look away. Turn and focus on something else. I can't. It feels like my eyes are glued to the red material around his neck. The tie that was used on me by the client was red. I bite my lower lip until it hurts and squeeze Pasha's hand.

"Mishka? Are you all right?"

I close my eyes, trying to suppress the memory of my

body being pressed into the bed while I desperately claw at the tie around my neck. My breathing becomes faster. Shallower. I can't get enough air. It feels like I'm suffocating.

"Asya?" Pasha wraps his arm around my waist and turns around, following my gaze. The guy with the tie is still standing next to the sunglasses rack, browsing through the display.

"Wait here, baby," Pasha says next to my ear and, releasing his hold on me, walks toward the man.

I thought he would ask the guy to leave. Instead, Pasha grabs the back of the man's shirt and pushes him toward the door. The man flails, yelling. Pasha pays him no heed, twisting the guy's arm behind his back while continuing to push him toward the exit. The store employee behind me lets out a shriek and grabs the phone, probably to call security. I fist my hands, hating myself for being so weak, then take a deep breath and march out of the store to where Pasha is still clutching the man by his shirt.

"Pasha," I whisper and wrap my hand around his forearm. "Please."

He looks down at me, releases the guy and pushes him away. The man stumbles, then turns around, biting out obscenities in our direction. Pasha takes a step toward him, but I tighten my hold on his arm.

"Please, don't," I say. "Let's go back."

He glares at the tie-clad man for a few more seconds before he takes my hand in his and leads us down the hallway toward the elevators.

As we're passing a restaurant, my eyes fall on the small object sitting atop the raised platform beyond the entrance to the establishment. I stop in my tracks, my feet seemingly rooted to the ground, and stare at the instrument.

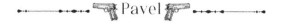

Pavel

I glance at what has caught Asya's attention, and my eyes fall on the piano next to the wall. It's one of those tiny versions—a baby grand piano made of white wood. Its lid is open and some music sheets lie on the small stand above the keys. The bench seat before it is unoccupied.

Asya takes a tentative step toward the platform and stops for a second. The next moment she's rushing forward, pulling me with her. When she reaches the piano, she releases my hand and climbs up to sit on the bench in front of the instrument. She sits there for at least five minutes with her eyes glued to the keys. I stand close by, turned in a way that allows me to keep an eye on her while I can still see our surroundings just in case someone gets a stupid idea of approaching and asking her to leave. One of the waiters looks up and takes a step in our direction. I cross my arms and turn toward him, daring him with my glare to say something. The man sizes me up but quickly goes back to what he was doing. Good for him.

A single low note plays behind my back. Followed by another. A few seconds of silence and then a melody begins. My body goes stone-still as a combination of low tones unfolds behind me in a slow tempo. The tune sounds familiar. It's a popular classical piece, but I can't remember which one. I want to turn around and watch her play, but I'm afraid it'll distract her. Instead, I stand guard, watching the people at the tables around us. All of them have stopped what they were doing, their meals abandoned as they all look in Asya's direction. The melody ends, but she continues with another. I know this one. It's "The Flight of the Bumblebee." Unbelievably fast. Even to a layman's ear, it's clear that she's not an amateur.

I can't fight the urge any longer. The need to see her play is too strong, so I turn around and stare. She might just be wearing plain blue jeans and a navy blouse, but it feels like I'm in a damn concert hall, watching the star pianist putting on a show. The way she holds her body, the movements of her hands flying elegantly over the keys, and the confidence in her posture are all stunning. But what takes me aback the most is the expression on her face. Joy. Elation. Happiness. She is smiling so widely that it feels like her whole being is glowing. I can't move. I can hardly breathe. Seeing her like this is as if I'm meeting her for the first time. There's nothing in common between this maestro and the frightened girl I let stay in my place, the one who still follows me around the apartment, gripping the hem of my shirt in her hand.

Rage boils up through my insides at the thought of this side of her being smothered. I'm going to make the people who broke her spirit pay. In blood.

Asya finishes the melody and looks up, her eyes finding mine. Applause breaks out around us. People are shouting, asking for more. She ignores the noise, slowly rises, and walks toward me without breaking eye contact.

"You didn't tell me you can play the piano." I reach out and move a few stray strands away from her face. She is still standing on the platform, which makes us almost the same height.

Asya just shrugs and takes another step forward,

plastering her front to mine. Our faces are barely inches apart.

"Which piece was it?" I ask. "The one you played first."

"Beethoven." She lifts her hand and traces the line of my jaw with the tip of her finger. "It's called 'Moonlight Sonata.' It reminds me of you."

The light falling through the window to the right of us makes her hair glow. A small smile still lingers on her lips. I fight the urge to bury my hands in her dark hair and crush my mouth to hers.

"We should get going," I say but I don't make a move to turn away. "It's almost noon. It's going to get crowded."

Asya's hand slides down from my face, grazing the sleeve of my jacket until her fingers wrap around mine. Her skin feels so soft compared to the roughness of my palm.

"Can we come again tomorrow?" she asks peering deep into my eyes. "I've missed playing."

As if I could say no to her when she's looking at me like this. "Sure, mishka."

A huge grin spreads over her face, making me feel like I'm bathed in its warmth. I want more of it. More of her. I reach out and place my hands on her hips. "Want to hop up?"

She tilts her head to the side, regarding me.

"Looks like a business group just arrived," I lie, then nod toward the left side of the hallway. "They just went into one of the stores."

Asya's hand squeezes mine, and she jumps into my arms the moment after. Her legs wrap around my waist, and she tucks her nose into the crook of my neck. Ignoring the stares of the people around us, I turn and walk toward the elevators, supporting Asya with one hand under her thighs, my other arm wrapped around her middle, holding her tightly against my body.

I should feel bad for lying to her, but I don't. The satisfaction I feel from having her body pressed to mine overwhelms any remorse I might have. I know it's selfish, but I don't fucking care.

CHAPTER
eleven

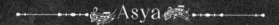

Asya

THERE ARE TWO CARTONS OF MILK INSIDE THE fridge. The regular one and one that's fat-free. Pasha usually buys only the regular full-fat milk. I squeeze the fridge handle and glare at the cartons sitting there so innocently on the shelf. They mock me.

It's fucking milk!

A palm caresses the small of my back. "Problem with the milk?"

"Yes," I say, staring the damn things down. "Was there a two-for-one special on milk at the store?"

"Nope. I bought skim this time too in case you like it more than the other one." Pasha stands behind me and touches my elbow, then trails his hand down my forearm until his palm presses over the back of my hand. Slowly, he lifts my hand to the shelf where the milk cartons are. "Which one do you want?"

"I don't know."

"Of course you do." He moves my hand a little further

until my fingers touch the top of the first carton. "I've never liked skim milk. It tastes almost like water. You?"

"I don't like the skim one, either." I blurt out without actually thinking about it.

"There. It wasn't that hard." He moves my hand to the other milk option. "We'll go with this one. You can make some oats cereal for me, too."

His hand falls away, leaving mine hovering just over the cartoon. I grab it and take it off the shelf. "Last time we had it, you said it tasted like cardboard."

"I'm ready to give it another try."

I turn around and look up at him, enjoying seeing him clearly through my new glasses without having to squint to gain focus. The ability to take in every line of Pasha's face surpasses the satisfaction of being able to see everything else around me in striking detail.

A few strands of his wet hair have fallen across his forehead. I try to sweep them away, but they keep sliding over his eyes.

"You need a haircut," I say as I try one more time.

Pasha cocks his head to the side, regarding me, then pulls out a drawer on his left. His eyes remain locked on mine while he rummages around in the drawer and pulls out a pair of scissors, placing them on the counter. They're huge, with white plastic handles. I use them to open pasta packages and other stuff.

"Those are paper scissors," I say, staring at them.

"I know."

He wants me to cut his hair. I move my gaze back to his striking gray eyes. "I've never cut anyone's hair, Pasha. What if I mess it up? Don't you have a hairdresser or a barber who could do your hair?"

"I do. But I'd like you to do it," he says and brushes my cheek with the back of his hand, "Will you?"

My heart skips a beat. I put the milk down on the counter and pick up the scissors. Pasha turns and leaves the kitchen. Two minutes later he comes back carrying a chair in one hand and my pink comb in the other. He places the chair in the middle of the kitchen and sits down with his back to me.

I walk toward him on shaky legs while my heart accelerates to double time. When I'm behind him, he lifts his hand, holding up the comb. I bite my bottom lip, accept the comb, and start passing it through the dark blond strands. His hair is not very long, I would just need to shorten the part on the top of his head that's grown out a little. Instead of starting the cut, however, I keep brushing his hair. Pasha doesn't move a muscle, but I hear his loud inhale when I use my other hand and push my fingers through the strands. I pull up some of the longer hairs, cut off half an inch, and continue running my fingers through.

"I need to go out for a few hours," he says in a clipped voice and leans his head slightly back, closer to my touch. "Yuri's funeral."

"Okay." I nod and make another cut.

"I'll need to wear a suit. I'll change in the other room. You can stay in the bedroom until I've left."

I bend my head slightly and inhale his scent before I shift my hand to the next patch of hair. "Were you close? You and your friend?"

He doesn't reply right away. When I look at his face, I see

that his eyes are closed and his lips are pressed into a thin line. "In a way," he says finally.

I finish the last cut and set the scissors and the comb on the counter. Pasha is still sitting with his eyes closed. Leaning forward, I rest my chin on his shoulder and brush his cheek with my own. "I'm so sorry you lost your friend."

His hand comes up and cups my cheek. "Everybody leaves, mishka. One way or another," he says, stroking the side of my face with his thumb. "It's only a matter of time."

I watch him as he stands up and leaves the kitchen, carrying the chair with him. There was a very strange tone in his voice when he said that last sentence. As if he was referring not only to his friend who died.

CHAPTER
Twelve

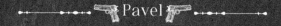
Pavel

I HATE FUNERALS.

    I guess everybody does, but they disturb me on a fundamental level. The expressions on people's faces. The sorrow. The crying.

    When they start lowering Yuri's casket and his sister breaks down, falling to her knees onto the muddy ground, I can't take it anymore. I turn around and head toward the parking lot while cries and pained screams ring out behind me. Even when I'm in my car, driving back home, I can still hear them in the recesses of my mind. The fact that we still have no clear proof of who's behind the attack makes it even harder to process.

    As I reach for the bell in my eagerness to hear Asya skirring to open the apartment door, I realize I'm still wearing the suit. I have a black coat over it, but it may still disturb Asya. I planned on taking a change of clothes with me but forgot. If someone told me a few months ago that I'd be concerned about not having some jeans and a T-shirt on hand, I would have laughed in their face. My loathing toward denim somehow got pushed away and dissolved since Asya's arrival. I know it's because wearing casual clothes instead of suits helps her, so I'm no longer bothered by the idea of tattered Levi's.

Pulling my hand back, I remove the coat and unbutton my suit jacket. Only when the jacket, vest, and shirt are all off do I reach for the bell again. A split-second later a thought slams into me that I should have just used my key. Too late.

Asya unlocks the door, opening it all the way. Her eyes go wide as her gaze moves down my naked chest and stops on my hand holding the bunched-up clothes. Slowly, she reaches out to take my other hand and ushers me inside.

"You'll freeze to death." She mumbles as she walks toward the living room with me following.

When we reach the couch, she lightly pushes me down to sit and disappears from view. I toss the bundle of clothes onto the other end of the couch and stare aimlessly at the blank TV screen. I still can't get the image of Yuri's sister sinking to her knees in the mud out of my head.

A light touch on my shoulder pulls me out of my daze as Asya comes to stand in front of me. She's holding a T-shirt and a gray hoodie in her hand. I don't leave my clothes lying around. She would have needed to go into the walk-in closet to get those for me. Where my suits are. I take the T-shirt from her and put it on. Once I have the hoodie on, Asya climbs onto my lap and wraps her arms around my neck.

"Was it bad?" she asks next to my ear.

I place my hand at the back of her head, threading my fingers into her hair, and inhale. "Yeah."

"Did you find out anything more about who the attackers were?"

"No. Just before he died, Yuri said they were Albanians, but we don't have any other info. The guy who supplied the drugs is dead. Without other leads, we can't make any connections."

Her hold on me tightens. I feel her chest rise as she takes a deep breath, then she starts whispering.

Asya

"The guy who took me wasn't Albanian. At least, I don't think he was." I say. My voice is trembling.

"Mishka, don't." Pasha places his palm on my cheek. "You don't need to talk about it if you don't want to."

"I was at a bar with my sister," I continue. "We used fake IDs to get in. All we wanted to do was go dancing. A guy approached us. He was handsome. Charismatic. Made us both laugh. He didn't have an accent; I would have remembered if he did. Sienna decided to go home early, she had Pilates the next morning. I stayed."

"Didn't you have bodyguards with you?"

"No. We snuck out of the house and took a taxi to the bar. Arturo always got furious when we did that."

His finger moves down to trace my chin.

"I thought he was funny. That guy," I say. "He said his name was Robert. We talked for an hour, and when I said I needed to go home, he offered to walk me outside to catch a cab. I found it very chivalrous."

It almost makes me laugh, how stupid I'd been.

"He pressed something over my face. A wet rag that

smelled harsh. I tried getting away, fighting him. He was bigger than me. Stronger. I lost consciousness soon after."

My voice is shaking. I close my eyes, willing myself to keep going.

"I came to in the dark. I was sprawled out on the cold ground and he was kneeling over me, tearing up my dress. I screamed and tried to fight him, but my mind was still hazy. Then I felt . . . him . . . between my legs." I tighten my arms around Pasha's neck and bury my face into him. His body is so utterly still, except for his chest that's moving due to fast, shallow breathing. "It hurt. So much. It was my first time."

I feel his arms coming around my back and press me into his body. It makes me sick, talking about this, but now that I've started, I can't stop. As if it yearns to get out of me. "I froze. I couldn't move my arms or legs; it was as if I was suddenly paralyzed."

The feeling of utter helplessness, the horror I felt in that moment . . . I don't think I will ever be able to forget.

"After . . . I managed to get away from him and ran toward the street. I ran as fast as I could. He caught me anyway. And then he drugged me," I say. "I woke up alone in a strange room. I was so so scared."

The arms around my body tighten, and I feel his palm stroking my back, just like that first night.

"There was a woman. Dolly. She was the one who gave me and the other girls the pills. And kept bringing them twice a day. She was also the one who instructed the girls and set up the appointments with . . . clients." I tilt my head up until my lips come right next to his ear and whisper, "I didn't fight it. I let them drug me and do whatever they wanted with me.

What kind of miserable, disgusting person do you need to be to allow that?"

Pasha's hand comes up to the back of my head, and he tilts my head until our eyes meet. "A young, innocent woman who was so violently abused that her mind shut down in an attempt to shield her. But you fought. Escaped. Survived. It wasn't someone else who saved you. You did it yourself."

"It doesn't make me feel any less disgusting."

"Don't say that, baby." He leans forward and places a kiss on my forehead. "I will find the people who hurt you. And they will scream for mercy as I break them like they tried to break you. Their deaths will not be quick."

My insights twist as I absorb his words. Do I want them dead? I imagine Robert as he pleads for his life. Bile rises in my stomach. But did I not plead also? And what about other girls? Now, as I picture Robert's screams for mercy, a small smile breaks across my lips.

"Can I watch?" I ask hesitantly, simultaneously dreading and craving the idea.

"Every second of it, mishka."

I lower my head onto Pasha's chest and wrap my arms around him. Uncertainty and wariness consume me. "I'm scared," I whisper. "I'm afraid it'll happen again. I don't know if I'll ever be able to go outside and walk down the street by myself without flinching every time someone passes close to me."

"You will." He resumes stroking my hair. "I promise you that."

Chapter Thirteen

Asya

"I HOPE THEY'LL LET ME PLAY AGAIN," I SAY AS I'M walking next to Pasha toward the car.

My anxiety spiked every time I thought about returning to the mall and being among all those people, the noise, and surrounded by all those smells. The memories caused me to shudder. But I also remembered the feeling of utter freedom that engulfed me when I placed my fingers on the keys after so long without music. All the excitement, joy, and happiness I didn't think I would ever feel again came rushing back. I've managed to stifle the need to play again for the past five days, but now I crave it.

I finally caved this morning and asked Pasha to take me over there.

"When did you start playing?" he asks as he fires up the engine.

"I was five. Arturo was trying to find a way to distract me and my sister from what happened to our parents, so he asked a neighbor, who had a piano, to give us lessons." It's hard to think about my brother and sister, knowing how much they must be worried, but the idea of facing them still leaves me with bone-chilling panic.

"What happened with your parents?" he asks.

"There was a raid on one of the casinos where they worked. Someone took out a gun and shot at the police. Then, everything went to hell. A lot of people were killed that night."

"They both died?"

"Yeah." I close my eyes and relax in the seat. "I can't even remember them that well. There are photos, of course, so I know what they looked like. But I can't remember details about them, and if I do, they're fuzzy. I remember my mom singing to us every night before bed, but I can't recall the song."

Pasha brushes the back of his hand down my cheek, and I lean into it. His light touch is there one moment and gone the next. When I open my eyes, he's putting the car into drive.

"I know what you mean," he says as he backs out of the parking spot. "I don't remember my parents, either."

"They died, too?"

"Maybe. Maybe not."

I watch his hard profile, wondering if he'll elaborate. He doesn't, just keeps driving in silence. I look down at his hand holding the stick shift and notice he's gripping it hard. I stroke his white knuckles with the tips of my fingers until I feel his hold loosen.

"Did you play professionally?" he asks after some time.

"No, not really. I played at school a couple of times, usually when we had a celebration. Music has always been something personal for me. I decided to take a year off after high school to figure out what I wanted to do next. I thought about applying to a music conservatory, but that was . . . before."

"Do you still want to?"

I look at the road beyond the windshield. "I don't know."

The elevator dings. I squeeze Pasha's hand and try to bring my breathing under control. The urge to ask him to go back clashes with the need to feel the keys beneath my fingers once again. The doors open. Pasha steps out, turns to face me, and takes both of my hands in one of his.

"Breathe. We'll go slow," he says and takes a small backward step. "I'm here. No one will dare touch you, mishka."

I nod and step out of the elevator.

There are more people around than there were the previous time. A multitude of sights and sounds overwhelm my senses—lights, laughter, footsteps, children running by while their parents are frantically trying to corral them. I close my eyes.

Pasha's rough palm cups my cheek and his thick arm wraps around my waist. "It's okay, baby."

My eyes flutter open and I take a deep breath. Hooking my fingers through the loops of his jeans I look up at him. His head is bent, barely inches from mine.

"You like music," he says. "Let's make this a dance. Almost like a waltz, yes?"

I can't help but smile a little. "People will laugh at us, Pasha."

"I don't give a fuck."

He takes a step back and I follow. Then another one. And another one. It does feel like some strange dance—him holding me close and walking backward—and suddenly, I feel the urge to laugh. So, I do. People around us must think we're nuts, but I don't care. I keep my gaze glued to Pasha's as I follow him, laughing. It's so good to feel joy again. He watches me with a small smile on his face and moves his thumb to my lips, stroking them.

"I wish you'd laugh more often," he says.

"I'll try."

When we reach the restaurant with the piano, he slowly lifts his hand off my face. I turn toward the corner where the piano should be, and my smile falls away. It's not there. Instead, two large flowerpots are in its place. I look around, wondering if they moved it somewhere else, but there's no sign of it.

"Can we get out of here?" I ask, staring at the flowerpots, trying my best to keep the tears at bay.

Pasha turns the key in the lock and opens the door to his apartment, holding it for me. I step inside, heading straight for the bathroom to splash some water on my face. As I cross the living room I come to a stop in the middle of the room. There, by the wall next to the window, is a small white piano. It's the one from the mall. I cover my mouth to stifle a sob.

"How?" I choke out, staring at the piano.

"I bought it last week and had it in a storage nearby, ready to be brought here when we headed out," Pasha says behind me, and I feel his hand on the small of my back. "I wanted to surprise you. You didn't even notice that we took the longer route back—to give the delivery guys more time."

"But, why?"

"Because you didn't feel comfortable at the mall. We will go again, only because you need to adjust to being in a crowd. But you should be able to play where you can enjoy it."

"Thank you," I whisper, pressing my lips together tightly. I want to turn around and kiss him, but I don't think he would let me.

"Will you play something for me?" he asks.

"Yes."

I take his hand and lead him across the room. He even bought the bench that was there with the piano. I take a seat on one end and pull him down to sit next to me.

Leaning forward, I pass the tips of my fingers over the keys, position my hands, and play. I pick one of my favorite modern pieces, Yiruma's "River Flows in You." It's soothing but strong, seductive, and full of emotion. It reminds me of Pasha.

He doesn't speak. Doesn't ask what I'm playing. He just sits there—big and silent—watching my hands as I move from one piece to the next. At some point, his gaze moves from my hands to my face and stays there.

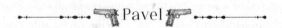

Pavel

For more than an hour, I sit on the bench next to Asya, listening to her play. Or better said, I stare at her while she plays.

I find it impossible to take my eyes off her face, seeing every emotion as it crosses her features. When she's playing a fast and uplifting piece, there is a wide smile on her face. When she switches to something slow and sad, her smile fades. She's not merely playing the notes; she feels and experiences every emotion as the melody gives and flows through her, lighting her up from the inside out.

When I'm finally able to unglue my eyes from her face and throw a look at my watch, I see that it's almost two. We've only had breakfast this morning, and while I don't have a problem with skipping meals, I don't want Asya to be hungry.

I rise off the bench and head to the kitchen in search of the takeout menu from the fast-food joint one block over, but I change my mind and open the fridge. I'm used to having it always nearly empty, so it's strange to see all the shelves packed full. Asya usually orders whatever she needs online with my phone, so I don't even know half of the items in there. I move a bunch of vegetables to the side and take out a package of chicken. Well, at least I think it's chicken. Asya's been preparing food for us every day, so I guess I could handle that task today. I find the frying pan in the cupboard and turn toward the island where she keeps her spices in a wide black basket. There are at least twenty small jars. I take one out and smell the contents. It's labeled as sage. Isn't that tea of some type? I put the jar back and pick up another. This one looks like salt, but it has some green things in it.

"Need help?" Asya's voice chimes behind me.

"You were playing. I wanted to make something for us to eat. I'm looking for salt. The normal kind." I turn around and find her smirking at me.

"So, you know how to cook?"

"I know how to heat the leftovers from takeout. Does that count?"

"That doesn't count." Asya laughs and I absorb the sound. I love when she laughs. "Come on, I'll show you how to prepare something simple."

She takes the jar out of my hand and opens it. Keeping her eyes on mine, she licks the tip of her finger and dips it inside.

"Here. Try it. It's just salt with herbs." She lifts her finger, holding it in front of me.

I stare at her. She's still smiling. Slowly, I take her hand and bring it closer to my mouth. Without removing my gaze, I lick at the tip of her finger, but I can't focus on the taste. All my attention is glued to Asya's face. She's biting her lower lip, looking at me with wide eyes. I take a step forward until our bodies touch. I can feel her chest rising and falling as her breathing quickens. Her free hand comes to land at the small of my back, then slides under the hem of my T-shirt. I can feel the heat of her touch. The urge to grab her, put her over my shoulder, and take her to the nearest bedroom is raging inside of me. Asya's palm moves up along my spine, and my mind is assaulted with images of her naked under me as I kiss every inch of her body. Just as I've been imagining for days. Wrong. So wrong.

I let go of her hand and quickly step back, turning toward the kitchen island. "What else do we need for this lunch?"

I don't miss the soft sigh as I hear her opening the cupboard behind me. "A bigger pan."

Asya walks around the kitchen, collecting everything she needs and cutting up the vegetables while my eyes follow her the whole time. I like having her here, in my space, way more than I should. Turning around, she opens the drawer next to me and reaches inside, but her hand falters. I look down and see that there are two different brands of flour.

"It's the same thing. Just a different manufacturer," I say.

"I know." She nods but doesn't make a move to take one.

For a few moments, I wait to see if she'll choose, but when I notice a look of frustration on her face, I take her wrist and move her hand toward the package on the left. "How about that one?"

"Thank you," Asya mumbles, takes out the flour, and walks toward the stove.

She's mad at me, but it's better this way. Even if there wasn't this age gap, we are from two completely different backgrounds. Giving in to temptation and letting something happen between us is out of the question. I'm already treading a thin line, and every day it's becoming harder to control myself. Sometimes, I wish she'd just call her brother to come and get her, because having her so close all the time, makes me feel like I'm going to combust. Just as often, though, I'm flooded with an urge to find her brother myself . . . and dispose of him before he has an opportunity to take her away from me.

CHAPTER
fourteen

Asya

CLUTCHING THE COAT AROUND ME, I STARE AT THE front door.

I've been looking at it for at least an hour. First, for ten straight minutes from the middle of the living room, then I managed two steps toward it and continued staring. It took me an hour of this stare-take-a-step-stare cycle to finally reach it. As I'm grabbing the handle, my hand is shaking. Biting at my lower lip, I open the door and exit the apartment.

Pasha's place is on the third floor, but since most of the residents use the elevator, the stairwell is vacant. Tiny shuffle at a time, I make my way down the stairs. It's quite a feat, considering how much my legs are shaking.

Pasha went to a meeting with his pakhan two hours ago, so he should be back soon. I could have waited for him, but I can't bear this feeling of helplessness anymore. I've been hiding in his apartment as if I'm a criminal for more than a month now, and I've finally decided I won't do it a second longer. I'm going to leave the building and take a walk around the block.

Alone. It's three in the afternoon; what could possibly happen? Just a small walk, a completely normal thing, and I'll go back. I've been outside several times with Pasha. I will be okay.

When I make it to the foyer, I wave to the security guy sitting behind his desk and head toward the exit. A big glass sliding door allows me to see people as they pass by on the sidewalk. As I approach the door, a wave of nausea comes over me and gradually becomes worse as I get closer. The door swooshes to the side. I swallow the bile and take the last few steps.

My feet reach the sidewalk. I stop and look up at the sky, feeling the sunrays on my face. It wasn't that hard.

Someone moves by me, catching my shoulder with their arm. I flinch and look to the side to see an older woman walking away. She rounds the corner and disappears from view. I'm feeling sick to my stomach and my hands and legs are still trembling slightly, but it's getting better now that I've finally crossed the threshold.

Laughter rings out across the street as a group of kids runs inside a building. To the left, there is a grocery store with a lot of people going in and out, so I decide to turn right. I'm almost to the corner when a taxi pulls over just ahead and a man steps out. I stop and watch as he gets a laptop bag from the back seat. He's wearing a black suit with a white shirt and a dark gray tie under his unbuttoned coat. My heart thumps at double its normal speed. My breath hitches. The taxi leaves and the man slings the bag's strap over his shoulder and heads in my direction. I take a step back. Then another one. The man keeps walking, and with each of his steps, my breathing becomes more erratic. I turn around and run.

People. Too many people. They are all looking at me. I

crash into someone's chest. Two hands grab my upper arms, probably just to steady me, but it feels like claws burying into my flesh. I scream and, the moment the hands release me, resume running.

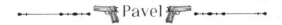

Pavel

"Did that waitress who's sleeping with Dushku find anything out?" Roman asks.

"No," I say. "Apparently, he talked about some confiscated shipment and complained about his wife spending too much money on shoes. But that's it."

"I've known Dushku for fifteen years. He's a master schemer and he's ruthless when it comes to business. But he would never get involved in human trafficking. If there's a connection here, we're not seeing it." He turns to Dimitri. "What about the men you have following Dushku's son-in-law?"

"Nothing."

Roman hits the surface of his desk with his palm. "What's the name of that guy Julian sends to do his errands? Besim?"

"Bekim," Dimitri says.

"That one. I want Mikhail to have a chat with him. Someone dared to send mercenaries into the Bratva club and kill our men just to silence a seemingly nobody. It means there is a lot at stake. We'll find out who's responsible for Yuri's death, and I will personally slaughter him."

"What if it was Dushku who orchestrated everything after all?" I ask.

"Then he will die. And it will be neither fast nor pretty. Has the girl staying with you said anything?"

"She said the man who grabbed her didn't have an accent. The name he gave her was Robert, but that could be a fake."

"I'll have Maxim get photos of Dushku's men. Would she be able to recognize him?"

"Probably."

"Good. When are you planning on taking her to her family? She's been at your place for a month."

My body stiffens. I've always been honest with Roman. Until today. "She won't tell me her last name or give me their number," I lie. "I have no way of finding them until she does."

"Perfect," he barks. "And how long do you expect to remain on this unplanned vacation? The clubs won't run themselves."

"I've taken everything I need from the office, and I've been working from home. Kostya has been personally handling whatever I can't do remotely."

"All right. But next Saturday I need you at Baykal. I have a meeting with the Ukrainians. They want an in with us."

"They got over the Shevchenko fuckup?"

"Everybody knows Shevchenko was an idiot. Sergei did them a favor by killing him." Roman shrugs. "They're sending a new guy to handle the talks. He's coming with two other men."

"Okay. I'll double the security."

He leans back in his chair and motions with his hand toward my outfit of jeans and a T-shirt. "What's with the new fashion style?"

"I needed a change," I say and see him lift an eyebrow. "Anything else?"

"No. You're free to go. Dimitri and I will go over the rest."

I nod and leave the pakhan's office.

As I'm heading down the hallway, the kitchen door on the other end bursts open, and a petite brunette in a paint-stained dress runs out. Her hands are laden with *piroshki,* and she is struggling to make sure none fall in her haste. At the top of the stairs, a little dark-haired girl starts jumping up and down and clapping her hands. Her sweet giggles echo off the hallway's high walls. Roman's wife and daughter. Nina Petrova sprints up the stairwell, nearly reaching the top when the kitchen door swings open again and Igor—the cook—wobbles out, shouting obscenities in Russian. If Roman catches him cursing in front of his little girl, the old cook will be as good as dead. I shake my head and stride toward the front door as the chorus of Igor's yelling and female laughter rings behind me.

"Mr. Morozov," the security guy in the hall of my building nods as I enter. "How was your day?"

"It was good, Bobby. Thank you."

"Oh, your girlfriend isn't back, yet."

I freeze in midstep. "What?"

"She left half an hour ago. I thought you'd like to know."

"Left?" I ask as panic floods my system. "Where?"

"I'm not sure. She just walked outside. I didn't see where she went."

I rush toward the security desk and come around to the other side. "Show me the camera feed from that time."

He skips the video to the moment when Asya walked

out. She stands on the sidewalk, in full view of the camera for a couple of moments, then goes to the right. A few minutes later, she runs past the entrance at breakneck speed. I can't see her face, but based on how fast she's moving, she was scared shitless.

"Call me if she comes back!" I bark and run toward the exit.

I rush along the sidewalk, frantically looking in all directions, but I don't see Asya anywhere. There is a grocery store nearby. I walk inside and ask the cashier if he saw a girl meeting Asya's description, but he only shakes his head. I leave the store and continue down the street, asking people if they saw her, going inside other businesses, but no one has seen a runaway girl. When I reach the intersection at the end of the street, I turn around and head back. It's too crowded here. I doubt she'd go into a big mass of people.

Dread and anxiety keep building within me with every passing minute. She couldn't have gotten far, so why can't I find her? I should have bought her a phone, so she could have called if she needed me. It didn't even cross my mind until now since we were almost always together. Idiot!

I spot a group of kids hanging around the steps in front of a building across the street, laughing, so I sprint toward them.

"Did you see a girl run by about five minutes ago?" I ask.

"Yellow coat. Long brown hair?" a kid of about nine asks.

"Yes." I nod.

"I think I saw her running there." He points toward the alley behind the grocery store. "She seemed scared."

I swivel around and run across the street, nearly getting clipped by a taxi, and dart into the narrow alley. It looks deserted at first glance, but I keep going deeper, passing the dumpster by the grocer's back door. The smell of rotten fruit emanating off the trash cans accosts me, reminding me of a time when the stink of spoiled food was all I could smell. I fist my hands and round the corner, moving between the buildings.

It's my fault. I should have taken Asya outside more often, a bit more every day so she could have gotten used to being around other people again. I should have insisted on her going to the shrink or tried harder to convince her to call her brother. She needs to get back to her life, to her family. I didn't do any of that. Instead, I let her hide in my place. With me.

I like waking up with her curled into my side—her small body pressed to mine as if even in sleep, she subconsciously sought my presence. Or how she climbs onto my lap when we sit down to watch TV in the evenings and rests her head on my shoulder. She usually falls asleep after ten minutes, but I stay on the couch for hours, and only when it's well into the night do I carry her to bed. It feeds whatever longing that's awoken inside me, the inner need to keep her engulfed in my arms all the time, to know she's safe where no one can ever hurt her again. She's been staying with me for more than four weeks now, but she still keeps following me around the apartment, holding either my hand or the hem of my shirt. It feels good to be needed. So, I stopped trying to convince her to call her family. The selfish son of a bitch I've transformed into wants to keep her.

The alley curves to the right and ends in a big concrete wall. A pickup truck is parked beside it. There's no one around. I almost turn to head back when I spot something yellow under the truck. I rush over and stop in my tracks. There, between the truck and the wall, Asya is laying on her side, her face toward the wall and her arms wrapped tightly around her middle.

"Jesus." I kneel and gather her into my arms. She's shaking. The moment I have her in my embrace, her arms envelop my neck, and her legs wrap around my waist. I place my palm on the back of her head, tucking her face into the crook of my neck.

"It's okay, mishka," I whisper. "I have you."

Asya

Pathetic.

Weak.

That's how I feel as Pasha carries me back to his apartment. I can't gather the courage to even lift my head and look up because I'm afraid I'll freak out again. Instead, I keep my face buried in his neck.

I don't understand why he keeps troubling himself with me. All I did was barge into his life and make a mess out of it. I've been dreading the moment when he'll sit me down and tell me it's time for me to leave. It's bound to happen, and probably soon. I'm nothing to him. I can't keep disrupting his life. But just the idea of leaving his side makes me shudder from the terror it unleashes inside of me.

"Let's get you showered," Pasha says as he carries me inside the apartment.

In the bathroom, he stops next to the shower stall, waiting for me to let him go. Instead, I cling to him harder.

"Asya, baby. Look at me."

Reluctantly, I lift my head from his neck and look into his eyes. I don't think I ever met someone with eyes like Pasha's—the color is a striking metallic gray.

"You need to wash your hair," he says in his deep voice, and it seems I can feel it all the way to my bones. "You have engine oil everywhere."

"Can you do it?" I blurt out and regret it the moment the words leave my mouth. As if he's not burdened enough with me already.

Pasha watches me for a few moments, raises his hand as if intending to place it on my face but changes his mind and just takes my glasses off.

"Okay." He sets the glasses next to the sink and slowly lowers me down.

I take off my coat and sweater, then remove my shoes and jeans. Pasha waits patiently in front of me, his eyes fixed on mine. Even when I shed my bra and panties, his gaze never wanders lower.

It should bother me, being naked in front of him. It doesn't. Just the thought of a man looking at my nude body usually makes the bile bubble up my throat. Any man except him. I wish he would look lower. Touch me. Kiss me.

I step into the stall and turn on the shower. Water hits me from above, the stream falling straight down onto my head, making the rivulets run down my body. I stand unmoving under the spray and watch as Pasha takes off his jacket, removes his shoes and socks, and steps into the shower fully clothed. He takes the shampoo bottle off the shelf, pours an amount three times larger than necessary into his palm, and looks down at me.

"Turn around," he says, his voice huskier than usual.

I face away from him and reach out to shut off the shower. Once the sound of water ceases, the only thing I can hear is Pasha's deep breathing. His touch starts at the top of my head as his hands massage my scalp. The beating of my heart picks up pace. He took his shampoo, not mine, by mistake. But I didn't stop him. I close my eyes and inhale, letting the scent of sage and citrus fill my nostrils. I don't think I'll ever be able to connect those two scents with anything other than falling asleep next to Pasha.

His hands disappear from my hair. I turn on the shower again and slowly turn around.

The water is cascading down my face, blurring my vision, but not enough to obscure the sight of his wide chest in front of me. His white T-shirt is completely wet and plastered to his body, revealing the images inked on his skin. He rarely removes his shirt in front of me. I think he believes his tattoos scare me. They don't. Nothing about Pasha scares me, just the opposite. The only time I feel absolutely safe is when he is with me.

I tilt my head up and find those gray eyes of his staring at me. God, I want to kiss him so much. I've been thinking about it for weeks, but can't decide if I should or not. Now, however, looking at him—all wet from head to toe because I asked him to wash my hair for me—I don't have to decide. There's no question if I want or not, only the need to feel his lips on mine. I raise my hands to cup his face with my palms and pull his head down.

"Asya." He bends slowly, looking into my eyes.

"I love how you say my name." I smile. He pronounces it with a Russian lilt. Lifting onto my toes, I tilt my head up and lightly touch my mouth to his. "Say my name again. I want to know how it tastes on your lips."

Pasha's hand comes to rest at the back of my neck, stroking the sensitive skin there, while his eyes bore into mine.

"Please," I whisper over his lips.

He touches his forehead to mine and closes his eyes. "You've been hurt."

"I know." I move my hand along his jaw and bury my fingers in his wet strands.

"You're eighteen," he says. "I'm too old for you, mishka."

I bite his lower lip lightly. "Bullshit."

His hand at the back of my neck grips my hair. His breath fans my face as he exhales, and he opens his eyes to look at me. "Asya," he says into my lips, then seizes them with his own.

I grab at the material of his wet shirt to keep myself steady as I let him devour me with his mouth.

"Asya," he says again between kisses, moving his lips to my chin and along my neck. "My little Asya."

I grab the hem of his shirt and pull it up and over his head. Pasha's hands glide down my body, stopping under my thighs as he lifts me. I wrap my arms and legs around him at the same moment, just as I have so many times before. The movement is so natural, it feels like I've been doing it all my life. He carries me out of the bathroom and toward the bed, kissing me the whole way.

"We won't do anything, mishka," he says and lowers me to stand next to the bed. "I will just be kissing you. Okay?"

I nod and brush my palm down his cheek. "Okay."

"I need to grab a change of clothes. Wait here."

Oh, so not happening. I jump back into his arms.

"Asya." He looks down at me. "I need to go into the closet, baby."

I know what he means. His suits are there. "I won't look," I say.

Pasha squeezes his arm around my back. "Okay. I'll be quick."

He runs. I don't even notice the suits because he just rushes inside, grabs a pair of boxer briefs, pajama bottoms, and a T-shirt, and he's out in under five seconds.

When he places me on the bed again, I drift to my spot next to the wall and pull the blanket over my naked body. My hair is still wet and will soak the pillow, but I don't care. Pasha turns his back to me and, in a few quick moves, changes out of his wet jeans and underwear into dry boxer briefs and pajama bottoms.

"Don't," I say when he reaches for the T-shirt.

He looks over his shoulder, then at the tee in his hand. "Mishka?"

"Please," I whisper.

Pasha nods and throws the T-shirt onto the recliner. The mattress dips as he climbs into bed. As soon as he's next to me, I lean forward and place a kiss on his naked chest. His hand comes under my chin, and he tilts my head up.

"Nothing will happen tonight. Just kisses and cuddling. But if you want us to stop, you need to tell me. Right away, Asya."

An urge to cry comes over me at hearing the words, but I bottle it up. Wrapping my arms around his neck, I crush my lips to his. His hand caresses my back, stroking me over the blanket. I shove the blanket off me and continue kissing him. Pasha's palm presses against the small of my back and, for a fleeting second, I freeze. He quickly removes his hand and lies there utterly still.

"It's okay," I say into his lips. "I know it's you."

He slowly puts his hand back, but it's barely touching me. I sigh, throw my leg over his waist, and climb on top of him. "Please, stop treating me as if I'm going to break when a wind blows in my direction."

Pasha's hand cups my cheek, brushing the skin under my eye with his thumb. "I'm afraid you're going to."

"You can't break something that's already been broken beyond repair, Pasha." I press my cheek into his palm. His jaw goes rigid and the vein at his temple pulses.

"We'll fix you up, mishka," he says through gritted teeth and pulls my face closer. "We will piece together every broken shard, I promise you. And then, we'll fucking annihilate the bastards who hurt you."

I crush my mouth to his. I don't think I'll ever go back to who I was before, but I don't tell him that. Only kiss him.

Pasha's arm circles my waist, and he rolls us until I'm on my back with his body looming over mine.

"Okay?" he asks, and I nod.

"Just kissing, and nothing else, Asya. Remember?"

When I nod again, Pasha slides down, his mouth landing on my collarbone and trailing a line down the center of my chest to my stomach. His hands roam over my arms, my sides—his touch slow and featherlight.

"No one will hurt you ever again, mishka," he whispers as he moves down my body, his lips covering every inch of my skin—down my right leg, then my left, all the way to my feet. As he shifts back up, leaving a trail of kisses along my inner thighs, that dreadful voice whispers inside my head.

You are disgusting. I don't know how he can stomach putting his mouth on something as filthy as you. The only thing you're good for is being fucked without mercy. You don't deserve any better.

I squeeze my eyes shut and move my hands down my body, pressing my palms over my pussy. Pasha's mouth stills on my hipbone.

"Baby? Do you want me to stop?"

I shake my head. "Please don't," I whisper. "Just not there."

"Okay. I won't do anything that will make you feel uncomfortable."

"It's not that," I say.

Pasha moves up my body and takes my face into his palms. "Give me your eyes, Asya."

I open my eyes to find him looking at me with concern. I don't deserve this. I don't deserve him.

"What did I do wrong?" he asks, and I feel the tears gathering in the corners of my eyes.

"You did nothing wrong," I choke out. "I just don't want your lips there."

"Why, baby?"

"Because . . ." I shut my eyes again and squeeze my legs together. "Because I'm dirty."

I feel the kiss land on my lips. "There is nothing dirty about you," he says. "You are the most beautiful, pure thing I've ever encountered, Asya"—another kiss—"and I will erase every bad memory you have, if you'll let me."

The tip of his finger traces along my eyebrow. "Please?"

"Okay." I nod.

Pasha takes my hand and places it on the back of his head. "Grab and tug it."

I bury my fingers in his hair and grip the silky strands.

139

"Harder, mishka," he says and nods when I do. "Good. I want you to do that the moment you want me to stop. Deal?"

"Yes"

He kisses my lips again before moving his mouth lower, to my chin, my neck, across my collarbone and over my breasts to my stomach, then he pauses. When I don't do anything, he slides even lower until his lips reach my pelvis, and he waits again, looking up at me. He's pausing to give me a chance to stop him, but I don't. I take a deep breath and nod.

A kiss lands at the center of my folds. Then another one. A pause. Two more kisses, and I shudder.

"Asya?"

"I'm okay," I mutter.

Another kiss. A tentative lick. Pasha's hands push on the inside of my thighs, opening my legs wider. In the next moment, his tongue presses to my clit. I inhale and shudder again as a tingling feeling unfurls in my core. Several more licks, and another kiss. His lips mold to my pussy and suck. A moan leaves me, and I squeeze at his hair without thinking.

Pasha's head snaps up. "Baby?"

"Sorry." I let go of his hair and push his head down between my legs again. "More."

He resumes licking me—slow at first, then faster. The pressure between my legs builds, but I need more. Pasha's mouth slips lower, his tongue entering me, and I gasp at the sensation. My body starts shaking.

"I need . . ." I mutter, arching my back. "More."

"Just my mouth today, mishka," Pasha says and moves to suck on my clit again. My body is trembling, yearning.

"More!" I scream and grip his hair with all my strength.

He keeps teasing my clit, switching between licking and

sucking while his hand moves along my inner thigh closer to my core. My breathing picks up the moment I feel his finger at my entrance, I'm already close to combusting. Slowly, his finger slides inside, so impossibly carefully, it makes me want to weep. He's acting as if it's my first time. As if there weren't dozens of other men who already plunged their way inside me by force. I throw my head back and moan, riding the unfamiliar feeling of floating that comes over me while wetness pools between my legs. When he has his finger fully in, he presses his lips over my clit and sucks, hard, and it feels like I burst into a million tiny butterflies. I never imagined that it would feel so whimsical to have an orgasm.

My body is still trembling when Pasha lies down beside me. He wraps his arm around my front, placing his hand on the back of my head, and tucks my face into the crook of his neck.

"I wish my first time was with you," I whisper.

"It will be."

"Pasha, you know very well—"

His hand covers my lips. "Your first time is going to be with me," he says next to my ear. "All that from before, it doesn't count. Do you understand?"

I press my lips together, trying not to cry while something warm swells inside my chest, gluing together a couple of the broken pieces of my soul.

CHAPTER

fifteen

— Pavel —

"**P**ASHA, *MA CHE FAI?*"

I look up from the spaghetti I was just going to place into the pot. Asya is standing on the other side of the kitchen island, staring at my hands in horror.

"You do not break spaghetti!" She walks around the island, shaking her head.

"They're too long. Can't fit into the pot," I say.

"No, no, no, you can never do that." She takes the spaghetti noodles out of my hands and throws them into the trash can in the corner. Then, heads to the cupboard, probably to get another package. She stiffens the moment she pulls the cabinet door open, her hand squeezing the handle as she stares at the bags of different pasta lined up on the top shelf. They are all different brands. I walk up and lift her free hand until it's hovering right before the bags.

"Take your time," I say next to her ear and let go of her hand.

Asya stares at the shelf. With her hand still hovering in midair, she bites her lower lip, then grabs the middle bag.

"I did it," she says, squeezing the bag.

"You did." I smile and place a kiss on the side of her neck.

She tilts her head, giving me more access.

"I'm so proud of you, baby."

"I never would have managed it without you." She turns to face me. "You know that, don't you?"

"You would have."

"No. I probably wouldn't." She places her hand on the back of my neck, pulling me down for a quick kiss. "Thank you."

She rushes around the kitchen, getting the pasta into the pot and the cheese out of the fridge. There's a small smile on her lips, and I feel the warmth in my chest upon seeing it. I'm so fucking proud of her. It took weeks of practice to get to this point, and she's doing considerably better. It may take us a little more time for us to be where she won't need me to steer her toward the decision, but we'll make it there eventually. Suddenly, panic replaces the warmth in my chest. Will she leave when she gets better? She probably will.

 Asya

"I should be back shortly," Pasha says as he walks inside the closet. "I need to sign some contracts and check if Kostya made another mess with the orders. If it happens to take more than two hours, I'll call you."

I look down at the phone in my hand. He went out

yesterday, saying he had an errand to run, and came back half an hour later with a white paper bag. Inside was a brand-new phone and a pair of headphones. He said those are in case I wanted to listen to music.

I leave the phone on the nightstand and walk across the bedroom, stopping at the closet threshold. Pasha is standing in front of the shelf on the left, rummaging through a stack of T-shirts. I let my gaze dart to the rack on the right side where dozens of his suits and dress shirts are hung in perfect color order, from black to light gray. Biting down on my lower lip, I enter and approach it. Slowly, I reach for the hanger with a charcoal gray suit. My hand shakes as I touch the elegant fabric, taking the garment off the loop.

"I think you should wear this today," I say and turn around to face him.

Pasha's eyes fix on the suit I'm holding to my chest and then move up until our gazes connect. "Baby . . . I don't . . ."

"Please." I extend my hand, offering the outfit to him. "It's you. I would never be scared of you, Pasha."

He regards me with concern in his eyes, but reaches out and takes the suit from me. I offer him a small smile and walk toward the far end of the rack where his shirts are hanging. I slide my fingers across the hangers until I reach one of the white shirts, then take it off and return to Pasha. He lays the suit on the shelf and takes the shirt from my hand.

He slowly puts the shirt on, his eyes glued to my face the whole time as if he's waiting for me to freak out. I'm certain that if he spots even the slightest trace of fear on my face, he'll have the shirt off in a second. But he won't see it. He will always be my Pasha, no matter what he wears.

Once he has the shirt buttoned, he waits a few moments

before reaching for the pants and putting them on. Finally, he grabs the jacket.

"Okay?" he asks.

I nod and smile. When he gets the jacket on, I reach out and straighten his lapels.

"One more thing," I say and turn to open the drawer behind me.

A variety of silk neckties in multiple colors are rolled and stuffed in small compartments within the drawer. My eyes skim over them until I find one that's the same shade as his suit. As I extend my hand to take it out, an image of me restrained on the bed flashes through my mind. My hand falters just above the tie. I push the memory away, replacing it with thoughts of Pasha. Pasha embracing me in bed, stroking my back. Pasha moving the cereal box closer to my hand, encouraging me to make a choice. Pasha carrying me safely home even though I was dirty and smeared in oil. Pasha washing my hair. Pasha kissing me. I wrap my fingers around the silky material, take the tie out, and turn around.

"Can I . . . can I put it on you?" I choke out.

He doesn't say anything, just bends and cups my face in his palms. There's a strange look in his eyes as they bore into mine—a mix of concern and wariness but there's awe, too. And pride.

I drape the tie around his neck and begin making the knot, looping the wide part over the thin one. My fingers are trembling, and the fabric slips from my grasp. I take a deep breath, pick up the loose end, and resume my work. When I'm finally done, I let go of the tie and look up. That's when I become aware that Pasha is still holding my face.

"You are the strongest person I know," he says and presses his mouth to mine.

The kiss is gentle as if he's afraid I'll get scared. I might be broken, but what's left of me is desperately in love with him. I don't want him to hold back on me. I don't want gentle. I want all of him. I fling my arms around his neck and jump, clinging to him as if he were a tree. His hold on me is instantaneous, supporting me while I pull down his face and bite his lip. Hard.

"I want you to make love to me," I say into his mouth. "And I don't want you to hold back."

"Okay, mishka," he says between kisses. They're still delicate.

"Pasha." I squeeze the hair at the back of his head. "No holding back. I need you not to hold back. Promise me."

"Asya, baby, I don't want to—"

I press my finger over his lips. "I don't want to feel broken when I'm with you. So, I need you to treat me as if I'm not. Give me everything you have. Please. Promise me."

Pasha's arms tighten around my waist. "I promise," he says and crushes his mouth to mine.

It's a whirlwind of hard, fast kisses and bites. Clashing teeth and dueling tongues. We are a tangled mess of lips and limbs. He's holding me so tightly pressed against his body that I'm certain no tidal force in the universe could tear us apart. And I'm marveling at every second of it.

A melody pops into my mind and plays in the background as we attack each other's lips in a frenzy. "In the Hall of the Mountain King" by Grieg. My arms around his neck tighten. We don't stop kissing as he carries me to the bedroom until we reach the bed.

"I need to take off my clothes," he says into my mouth and lowers me to the bed.

I nod, reluctantly releasing my hold of him. He removes his jacket first and lets it fall to the floor. The tie is next. I see the concern in his eyes as he reaches for it. Leaning forward, I brush the back of my fingers down his cheek. "You promised."

The tie falls down, too. His shirt and pants follow and, soon, he's standing in front of me completely naked. My mountain king.

Getting closer I press my lips to his. "Now, please help me take off mine."

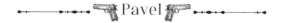

Pavel

I take a deep breath and circle my hands around Asya's waist. It doesn't matter what I promised. I can't make myself do anything that may lead to triggering her trauma, even if it means going back on my word. Focusing on her face, I hook my fingers in the waistband of her sweatpants and start pulling them down, inch by agonizingly slow inch. If I notice even a speck of distress, we're stopping. Then, I slide my palms up her legs, over her panties, and pull up on the hem of her top. She smiles and lifts her arms, shaking out her dark hair as the shirt comes free of her body. Unclasping the bra, Asya tosses it to the floor and stands in front of me, clad only in her panties. She tries to make herself look unfazed, but I see the restrained terror in her eyes. And also, the fierce determination to show me that she won't cave, no matter what I say. I caress her face and lean forward until we're nose to nose.

"You are the purest thing I've ever touched in my life," I say holding her gaze, "and I will never, ever hurt you."

"I know," she utters, then places her palms over mine and lowers herself onto the bed, pulling me down with her.

"Grab my hair, mishka."

Her right hand moves to the back of my head, fingers threading through the strands.

"Good. Now I need you to promise something," I say.

"What?"

"Even the smallest discomfort, you pull, and I'll stop."

"I promise."

I kiss her lips, along her chin, and down her neck. My cock is so hard it hurts, but I ignore it and continue peppering her body with kisses. Her small hand, arm, shoulder, across her collarbones to the other arm. I am going to erase every single evil touch she's had on her skin with my lips. When I reach her panties, I halt for a moment, waiting to see if she'll stop me. She doesn't. I trail a line of kisses from her midriff down, over her still-covered pussy, and back up to her stomach. Asya's free hand slides to the lacy material and pushes it down. I drop a kiss on the back of her hand, then take the sides of her panties and slowly pull them off.

"I will never hurt you." I lean forward and capture her slightly trembling lips with my own. "Hair, baby."

She takes a deep breath and takes a hold of my hair again.

"Never," I repeat, leaving a path of kisses from her neck all the way to her sex.

When I slide my tongue over her pussy, Asya's breathing picks up. I keep licking, then add my thumb and start massaging her clit. A small sound of pleasure leaves her lips, and I feel her wetness on my face. I quicken my licks and keep teasing her with my finger until I'm sure she's close, and then I suck on her clit. Asya arches her back and moans while the tremors pass through her body. Carefully, I lower myself over her, but keep most of my weight on my elbows. Her eyes flutter open, and our gazes connect.

"Yes," she answers my unspoken question and widens her legs a bit more.

I position my cock at her entrance, then slowly begin sliding inside. It's hard to hold back because the need to lose myself within her is overwhelming, but I keep my pace steady, half an inch at a time. And I don't break our eye contact the entire time.

Her breaths are coming fast, and her eyes are wide, but her grip on my hair doesn't waver. Once I'm fully inside, she gasps, her lips spreading into a smile. And then, the hold on my hair loosens and vanishes completely.

"Now, I need you to keep your promise," she says and kisses the side of my jaw. "I need you to treat me as if I'm not broken."

"You are you, mishka." I pull out, pause, and slowly slide back in. "Absolutely perfect . . ." I retreat, then slide inside again, but a little faster. "Just the way you are."

It's almost impossible to restrain my impulses, but I rein myself in and adjust the tempo so it builds slowly, making every thrust just a little bit faster and harder than the previous one. Asya's legs wrap around me, and she tilts her chin up, staring into my eyes.

"Prove it to me," she digs her nails into the skin of my arms. "Give me everything."

My control snaps in an instant. I bury myself in her to the hilt. Her body starts trembling under me.

"More," she chokes out.

I pull out and immediately thrust back inside, bottoming out in her heat.

"Faster!"

Grabbing the back of her neck, I pound into her—fast and hard—the sight of her flushed face etched forever on my mind. The bedframe creaks beneath us. I hook my fingers behind her knee, raising her leg and opening her more so I can slide in deeper. Asya's hands squeeze my arms, then move up to wrap behind my neck, pulling my head down for a kiss. I consume her lips like a starved man, taking more and more while rocking into her.

A moan escapes from Asya's delicate throat. I pull out completely and just watch her for a moment before slamming back inside. Her pussy spasms around my cock while her hot breath fans my face. She cries out as she comes. Hearing the sounds of her pleasure and seeing her come apart under me sends a jolt to my system, and I explode with a groan the very next moment.

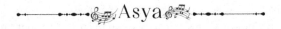

Asya

I'm in the room with the red drapes again. The heavy scent of male cologne clings to the air. My hands are tied to the headboard, and a huge male body looms above. Droplets of stinky sweat fall from his forehead onto my breasts. Pain spreads through my whole being as he thrusts into me again and again. I scream.

"Shh. It's just a dream," Pasha's deep voice says into my ear. "You're safe."

The panic recedes and extinguishes completely when he pulls me closer toward him, wrapping his arm tightly around my waist. I don't have nightmares that often anymore, but when I do, they are bad.

"Are you okay?" Pasha asks and places a kiss on my shoulder.

I flip around so I'm facing his naked inked chest. The lamp by the nightstand is on but dimmed, throwing a soft yellow light onto the black and red shapes. I reach out to stroke the line of a skull bathed in blood. It's one of many. There must be at least ten different skulls on his chest alone. The rest of the tattoos are of similarly disturbing scenes.

Most men in the Cosa Nostra have some ink. Even my brother has a full sleeve tattoo. But I don't think I know anyone who has their entire upper body tattooed like Pasha.

"Why so many?" I ask.

"Everyone has a different way of coping with the shit life throws at them. This was mine."

"What kind of shit?"

Pasha looks down at me and places the tip of his finger on the corner of my lips. "Abandonment. Low self-esteem. Loneliness," he answers, then looks away. "Humiliation. Hunger."

I blink at him in confusion. It's obvious he has money. His watch costs at least twenty grand.

"It wasn't always like this for me," he says, guessing my thoughts. He looks down at me again and traces his finger over my eyebrow. "I was left on the doorsteps of a church when I was three. The earliest memory I have is of a woman leading me up the steps to a big brown door and telling me to stay there. Then she left. It was probably my mother, but I can't be

151

sure. I don't remember what she looked like. I don't remember anything prior to those five stone steps and the brown door."

I slide my palm across his chest and examine the design on his left pec. It shows a dark double door. Thick black vines wrap around it several times as if to keep it shut. The details are amazing; the images are almost photo quality.

"You did that?" I point to the design.

"Yes. As well as most of the rest. Except for the ones on my back and other places I couldn't reach."

"Can I see those?"

He turns so his back is to me. Skulls again. Snakes. Lots of red. Spiders. Some strange, winged creatures. The style is similar to those on his front and arms, but they don't look as good as those he did himself.

"A jail buddy did those for me," he adds and turns back to face me.

My head snaps up and I stare at him. "You were in jail?"

"A couple of times."

"What for?"

"Police often raided the clubs where the underground fights were held. The charges varied from disturbing the peace to assault. I did four months for that last one."

"But you're so levelheaded. You even organize your T-shirts by color."

He smiles at me. "I organize everything by color, mishka."

I reach out and brush the side of his face with the tip of my finger. Such a hard-looking man. Yes, looks can be so deceiving, because his rough exterior hides an amazingly beautiful soul. How can someone who experienced the things he did have a heart as big as his? Is it big enough to include me, too? I lean forward and kiss him. The moment our lips touch, my soul begins to sing.

For as long as I can remember, I have associated music with the feeling of joy. Whenever I was feeling down or scared, I'd play the piano Arturo bought me. Sometimes, I played for hours until sadness or fear was replaced with joy. Right now, it seems that my relationship with music has transformed. I don't need to play anymore to feel better. I just need to be close to him, to my Pasha, and the melody fills me.

"How old were you when you started fighting?" I ask.

"Eighteen."

"Were you good?"

Pasha laughs into my lips. "Not in the beginning. The first few months, I got the shit kicked out of me."

"But you kept doing it?"

"The money was good. And as I got better, I earned larger sums. So I practiced every day and made sure I was the best I could be."

"So it was all about the money?"

"At first, yes," he says as he traces my chin with his finger, "but there was something . . . primal that rose within me when I heard people cheering and yelling my name. I got addicted to it, in a way. It was very fulfilling. Well, for a period of time, at least. I was twenty-three when I joined the Bratva. I can't believe it's been over ten years."

"So you went from a fighting ring to an upscale club. It's a big change."

"I started as a soldier. Sometimes running errands, but most of the time, I was sent to collect debts. I'd never even held a gun back then, so Yuri had to teach me how to shoot before I could be given more serious assignments."

"Do you like it? Running a nightclub?

"Two clubs, actually. I'm at Ural most of the time. It's a bigger one. The second club, Baykal, is mostly used to launder money. But yes, I like it."

I lean my head on his chest and stroke the inked skin of his stomach. "I've never been to a club. The New York Family isn't involved in the entertainment business, so Arturo only let me and Sienna go to bars owned by someone within the Cosa Nostra. And even that was rare."

"Why?"

"He was scared that something would happen to us. Sienna always wailed about how paranoid he was. I guess he was right to be."

Pasha's hold on me tightens, and he strokes my back.

"How does it feel?" His voice is soft, almost reverent.

"What?"

"To have a family. Someone who'll stay with you, no matter what. Even if you make a mistake. Even when you're angry. Someone who'll be in your corner even when they know you're wrong. To have someone who is . . . yours?"

The look in his eyes . . . I can't describe it. Longing. Hunger. And so much sadness.

"It's like warmth," I whisper.

"Warmth?"

"Yes. When you find yourself in a frigid, raging storm, they are the people who will do anything to make sure you don't get cold. They will wrap their arms around you, shield you, surround you in their own warmth while the icy wind beats on their backs."

"Is your family like that?"

"Sometimes, Sienna and Arturo are hard to deal with.

154

The three of us have very different personalities. But yes. They are both like that."

"Will you tell me about them?"

"Sienna is . . . a force of nature. She's loud. Outspoken. One moment, she would be laughing like crazy, and the next, she'd be crying her eyes out." A nostalgic smile spreads across my lips. "Sienna loves to pretend that she's shallow. She posts a gazillion photos on social media, wearing ridiculous clothes that usually make people think she's a bit whacky. Sometimes, she gives them the impression that she's not very bright."

"Why?"

"I have no idea." I reach out and trace the line of his brow with my finger. "My sister is the most intelligent person I know, but instead of doing something with her amazing mind, she'll just . . . fool around. The only thing that truly interests her is her writing."

"What does she write?"

"She's never shown me." I smile. "But I snuck a peek at some of her notebooks when we were younger. They were hidden in a box under her bed. She writes romance novels."

"Romance novels?" Pasha raises his eyebrow. "Is she good?"

"Yeah. Very good. Sienna has a thing with words. Other than English and Italian, she can speak four other languages. And she learned them on a whim."

"I don't think I've ever heard of anyone learning a language on a whim."

"My sister learned basic Japanese in a month, all on her own, just because a boy from school called her stupid." I laugh. "She was fourteen at the time."

Pasha smiles, but his eyes stay sad. "That's quite the

talent. Most people would be hard-pressed to learn and speak one foreign language, never mind five. I don't like speaking Russian. I understand it completely, but I almost never converse in it."

"I've noticed." I lean forward and press my lips to his. "Why?"

"Because I have an English accent if I do. None of the kids at the foster homes or schools spoke Russian, so during that time I kind of . . . just forgot it, I guess." He nips at my lip. "What about your brother?"

"Arturo is like all older brothers. Just a hundred times worse."

"Protective?"

"To a point of driving me insane. He was twenty when our parents died, so he took on their role."

"You didn't have any other family members?"

"We had an aunt. Dad's half sister. She offered to take me and Sienna in, to live with her. Arturo said no." I shake my head. "I'm worried about him. I think, something flipped in his mind when our mom and dad were killed, and he focused all his attention, outside of his work, on the two of us. He's thirty-three, but he's never brought a woman to our house. I know he had several relationships; we even met some of his girlfriends. But none of them have set a foot in our home. I think he was so focused on raising us that he actually forgot he's not really our parent."

"Why don't you want to call him? It's obvious he loves you."

"Because I love him, too," I whisper. "At first, I thought he wouldn't be able to get over what happened to me. So, I didn't want to call him."

"And now?"

"Now, I don't want to call because I know how much he'll hurt if he learns the truth. Arturo will put two and two together, even if I don't tell him everything. He'll blame himself. I can't allow that. He has enough on his shoulders, and he's shielded me from enough storms in my life." As I say this, something else crosses my mind. "There was a girl. At Dolly's place. I think she may have been Russian. She was brought in about a month after they took me, but she disappeared a few days before I got away."

His palm stills on my back. "Do you remember her name?"

"Rada, or something like that. I'm not sure. Why?"

"Could it have been Ruslana?"

My head snaps up. "Yes. It was Ruslana. Do you know her?"

"She was the daughter of one of the Bratva's soldiers."

"Was?"

"Her body was found around the time you escaped. A day or two earlier, I think."

I shudder and bury my face in the crook of his neck. She couldn't have been more than a year or two older than me.

"Will you be in trouble because you didn't go to the club tonight?" I ask, trying not to think about the girl with a long blonde braid and how it easily could have been me.

"I'll go tomorrow."

"Can I come with you?" I ask.

A kiss lands on the crown of my head. "Of course."

CHAPTER
sixteen

SOFT TONES OF A DELICATE MELODY REACH MY EARS as I exit the elevator. I walk up to the door of my apartment and pull the keys out of my pocket. Lately, I've been pretending that I've forgotten my keys so I can ring the bell and hear Asya's hurried steps as she runs toward the door to let me in. When she opens it, it's as if she has missed me, even though I've only been gone for a short time. It feels good to come home and know that she is waiting for me. So, I keep pretending to forget my keys and ring the bell each time.

But I don't want to distract her from her playing today. Opening the lock, I walk inside. Asya is sitting in front of the piano, her phone is on the small stand above the keys. She probably found new sheet music online and downloaded it. I should buy her actual sheet music books. It can't be easy to follow along on that small screen. Trying my best not to make any noise, I leave the grocery bags by the door and walk into the living room. I lean my shoulder on the bookshelf on my right and watch her.

Her hair is loose, and it sways left to right when she bobs her head along with the melody. I can't see her face from my spot, but I'm pretty sure she's smiling.

Something squeezes in my chest. Will she take the piano with her when she leaves? Because she will leave, eventually. I won't delude myself into believing she'd want to stay with me when she has a home, a family, probably a bunch of friends, and plans to attend a music conservatory. Her life might have been placed on hold with what happened to her, but she'll bounce back. I've seen her strength and determination. Her courage. All those things that make her *her*—the same traits that made me fall so desperately in love with her, they will also take her away from me.

We need to get to the club soon if we want to arrive before the opening and avoid the crowd, but I can't make myself ask her to stop. The melody changes as she switches to my favorite one, "Moonlight Sonata." I'm not sure why I love hearing her play that one the most. Maybe because of the first time I heard her play. I've even set it as her ringtone on my phone. I grip the back of my neck in frustration. I hope she takes the piano when she leaves. Because if she doesn't, I'm going to smash it until there is nothing left of it.

Asya

"If you get uncomfortable, even a little bit, let me know and we'll leave. Okay?"

I nod and squeeze Pasha's hand.

As we walk toward the entrance of the club, I look up at

the dark sky, searching for the small white flakes. The temperature has dropped significantly, and there is a crisp feel to the air. It's been clinging to my senses since the moment we left Pasha's building, along with the panic that's been rising in my chest. I almost asked Pasha if I could return to his place, fearing that it would start snowing. I thought I was getting better. In some ways, I was. But the idea of seeing the frost-covered ground makes my heart pound at double its normal rhythm.

A man standing at the entrance opens the door for us when we approach. He's wearing an unbuttoned black coat, revealing a black suit underneath. I tighten my hold on Pasha's hand and will myself to offer the bouncer a small smile as we pass.

Pasha leads me across the spacious area decorated in shades of black and gray. Tall tables surround the edges of a currently empty dance floor. Along the wall, a raised platform holds several large booths containing luxury leather seating. The space is completely empty, save for a girl who is cleaning at one of the booths, making the sound of our footsteps echo off the walls.

Finally reaching the opposite side of the floor, we climb the stairwell to the upper level. This space has been made to look like a gallery of sorts. The floor-to-ceiling glass wall leans out over the dance floor, exposing the entirety of the club's interior to anyone standing up here. We enter a room where a man in his early forties sits in front of a block of monitors showing various camera angles of different areas in the club. Pasha nods at the man and heads toward another door on the right.

As we enter, I spot a blond man in his twenties sitting behind a desk covered with papers. He's mumbling something to himself while glaring at the computer screen in front of him. His longer-cut hair is tousled but it doesn't hide the fact he's very handsome. A few months ago, my face would have flushed red if I saw him. But that was before I met Pasha. This guy may be attractive, but his looks have no impact on me.

"I see you finally decided to drag your ass here," the man grumbles then looks up from the screen, his eyes zeroing in on me and going impossibly wide.

"Kostya, this is Asya," Pasha says and leads me around the desk until we're standing in front of his friend. "Where are the contracts that need my signature?"

Kostya's gaze drops to my hand clasped in Pasha's before it flips back up to my face. His eyebrows shoot all the way up to his hairline.

"Eyes on me, Konstantin!" Pasha barks.

"Jesus fuck, man!" Kostya cringes. "Don't do that. Only my *babushka* calls me by my full name, usually when I've fucked something up."

"Contracts. Now."

"What the fuck has gotten into you? Did you change your fucking personality along with your wardrobe? Christ." He grabs a stack of papers out of the drawer and tosses them on the desk in front of Pasha. "Here."

Pasha starts signing the contracts, but his left hand retains its hold on mine the entire time. He's wearing jeans and a black sweater today. I tried to convince him to put on a suit, but he said no.

Kostya pretends to be busy with something on the computer screen, but I notice him throwing a quick look at me every few seconds.

Once Pasha is done signing, he pushes the papers to the center of the desk and straightens. "Is that all?"

"Yup."

Pasha nods and heads toward the exit. I wave at his friend and follow. We're at the threshold when Kostya calls out, "Oh, Pasha! You may want to drop by the old warehouse later."

"What for?"

"We've caught one of Julian's men. Bekim. Mikhail will be questioning him."

Pasha's body stiffens. He turns slowly and looks at his friend. "Call Mikhail. Tell him he can stay home with his family tonight."

"What? So, who's going to have that chat with the guy?"

Pasha looks down at me. "I will."

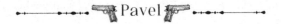

Pavel

When I enter the warehouse, Kostya is already there, leaning against the wall and fumbling with his phone. In the opposite corner, with his face to the floor, lies a man in his early thirties. His legs are bound with silver duct tape around his ankles and knees. His hands are tied behind his back. A dirty rag protrudes from his mouth.

Even after all these years, a faint scent of burned wood still lingers in the air. This is one of the warehouses that the Italians tried to burn down before we signed the truce. The basement in the pakhan's mansion has been out of commission since then—his wife doesn't appreciate the smell of blood in her house—so we decided to leave this warehouse as is and conduct our interrogations here.

I glance at the soldier standing a few paces from "our guest" and tip my head toward the exit. "Leave. I'll call you when I'm done."

The man nods and heads outside.

I don't waste any time and grab Julian's man by the back of his jacket, dragging him away from the wall to give me more room. He whines and starts thrashing, then moans when I let his body fall back to the floor. I place my foot on his back and wrap my hand around his thumb. The sound of bones breaking is followed by a muffled, pained whimper. I press my foot harder and take the next finger.

"You need to ask Mikhail to give you a quick course in torture," Kostya says from his spot by the wall. "The rule is: ask questions first. Then start breaking shit."

Another snap.

"Our methods differ," I say as I continue.

Once I've broken all ten fingers, I leave the man to weep on the ground and pick up a knife off the nearby table. I step on his back again and cut the tape binding his wrists. The man thrashes, trying to wriggle free. I grab his right forearm with one hand, his palm in the other, and twist them in different directions. The man screams around the rag as his wrist snaps. I repeat the action with his other arm.

I consider breaking his ankles next but decide I don't want to risk him passing out on me. Moving my foot to his side, I push at his body until he's facing up and yank the rag out of his mouth.

"Is Dushku distributing the new drug?" I ask.

"No," the man chokes out. "It's Julian. His son-in-law."

"Is Julian involved in the high-end prostitution ring, as well?"

"Yes. He's running it."

"Does Dushku know?"

He shakes his head and whimpers. I place the sole of my shoe on the broken fingers of his right hand and put pressure into my step.

"He doesn't know! It's all Julian and some of his college friends!"

"What do you know about the Russian girl who was found dead a few months back? She had your drug in her system."

"It was an accident," he wails. "A client got too rough, and she died. We had to get rid of her, and make sure she wasn't linked to us through the drugs we use. So we pumped her full of heroin."

I press my heel on his throat, enjoying the choking sound that leaves his mouth. "You will give my friend here the names and addresses of everyone who's involved in this scheme. Including the clients. Even the fucking janitor. Make sure you give the details about the woman—Dolly—in charge of the girls, too. And the address of where you're keeping them."

He nods.

"I also need the names of the men abducting the girls."

"Robert is in charge of that," he squawks when I ease my foot off a little.

Robert. The motherfucker uses his real name when luring the girls.

"American?" I ask.

"Yes. He's been working for us for the last three years. Julian brought him in."

"Last name and address."

He rattles off the information, and I commit it to memory.

"Kostya," I call. "Our guest is ready to talk. Come here to take notes and relay everything he tells you to Maxim."

I throw one last look at the man on the floor. "If you happen to forget a name, I will come back and finish what I started. And I'll make sure you stay alive and coherent until I'm completely done."

Leaving the warehouse, I call Asya to let her know I won't be back for another couple of hours. Inside the car, I enter the address Bekim gave me into the navigation system.

Seems like I'll be having another chat tonight.

CHAPTER
seventeen

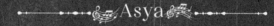 Asya

I WAKE UP TO THE FEELING OF FINGERS COMBING through my hair. Pasha is lying on the bed next to me, still wearing the same clothes he had on the previous evening.

"When did you get back?" I ask.

"Five minutes ago," he says and continues stroking my hair. "I need to show you a photo of someone."

"Okay." I nod. He'd already shown me photos of more than a dozen men the other day, asking if I recognize anyone, but none of them seemed familiar.

Pasha releases my hair and reaches behind him to take his phone off the nightstand. I take the phone when he holds it out to me and look down at the screen. The image is of a man suspended upside-down from a ceiling. I can't make out his face too much, so I zoom in. The phone nearly slips from my hand.

"Is this him? The one who took you?" Pasha asks. His voice is strained as if he's speaking through gritted teeth.

I swallow the bile that has suddenly risen up my throat. "Yes."

Pasha nods and takes the phone from my hand. He grasps my chin between his fingers, tilting my head up until our gazes meet. "We've got all the names. Everyone who was involved. The Bratva will deal with the rest of their organization, but I told Pakhan that this one is mine." He leans forward and presses his forehead to my own. "You said you wanted to watch."

"What?"

"Him, dying. Slowly. As I cut him piece by little piece."

I look into his gray eyes as they stare back at me and take his face between my palms. "Yes."

Pasha nods. "I'm going to shower and change. And then we'll leave."

It's a two-hour drive west of the city to a rundown house that's not much more than a shed. Pasha parks the car and turns toward me, taking my hand in his.

"If you've changed your mind, I'll drive you back," he says. "It's okay if you can't handle seeing that motherfucker again. I'll come back tonight and take care of him."

I look through the windshield at the house. The man who destroyed my life and messed up my mind is beyond that wooden door. Panic started brewing the moment I saw his image on Pasha's phone and multiplied tenfold during the drive here. The idea of seeing him again makes me sick, but I need this. I need vengeance. Maybe seeing him die will help me get myself back.

"I'm ready," I say.

The first thing I notice when Pasha opens the door of the house is the stench, a mix of vomit and piss. It's so foul, I barely manage not to immediately empty the contents of my stomach. It's dark inside. The windows are covered with shaggy drapes or nailed-on boards, and the only illumination is from the sunlight coming through the open door. I follow Pasha as he takes two steps to the left, squeezing his hand with all my might. There is a click when he flicks on the light. It's a small sound, barely audible, but in my head, it reverberates like an explosion. I want to turn around and look the asshole in the face, but I can't make myself move.

"It's okay, mishka." Pasha wraps his arms around me and presses my face into his chest. "He can't hurt you anymore. And I'll make sure he doesn't hurt anyone else, ever again."

I inhale deeply, savoring Pasha's scent. It's the scent of safety. And love. It would be so easy to ask him to kill the son of a bitch for me. But deep inside, I know I need to play this tune myself.

"Do you have a gun?" I mumble into Pasha's chest and feel him go still.

"Yes."

"Can I have it? Please."

His hold on me loosens, and his hands travel up my arms until they reach my face.

"You don't have to do this. I'll make sure he suffers."

I lift my hand and cup his cheek. My Pasha. Always ready to fight my battles for me. "Please."

He closes his eyes for a second, reaches into his jacket, and takes out a gun. "Do you know how to shoot?"

"No."

"Okay. Hold it like this." He places the weapon in my hand and moves my fingers to the correct position. "The safety is on. When you're ready, you switch it off. Here. You need to hold the gun tightly. This one has a bit of a recoil."

I stare at the handgun. It's heavy. Much heavier than I expected. I swallow and turn to face the man who ruined my life.

He's still in the same position as I saw in the photo. His feet are tied to the beam above, his arms are dangling. Something is wrong with them, however. They hang at an unnatural angle. It's hard to believe this is the same man I met at the bar. His dirty clothes are torn in several places. Dried blood is smeared over the exposed parts of his body, staining his shirt, and the floor below. His eyes are closed and one side of his face is swollen. He's not moving. I'd think he's dead already, but I can see his chest rising and falling.

I've imagined this moment so many times. Dreamed about making him pay for every fucking second of my pain. I thought that if I ever got the opportunity to avenge myself, I would want him to suffer as I did. But now, seeing him like this, I just want it to be over.

I cover the distance between us in quick steps until I'm standing right in front of him. His head is level with my chest, and the foul smell is even worse up close.

"I hope you burn in hell," I choke out and spit into his face. Robert's eyes flutter open, meeting mine. I flip the safety switch and press the barrel to the bridge of his nose.

And pull the trigger.

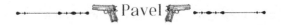 Pavel

A loud bang erupts through the room.

I wrap my left arm around Asya's middle, pulling her out of the way so the dead man's body won't hit her when it swings back. I don't think she even noticed me standing right behind her. I take the gun out of her hand, sliding the safety on, and carry her out of the house.

When we reach the car, I throw the gun onto the back seat and lower Asya to the ground, turning her to face me. Her hand and the sleeve of her yellow coat are covered in blood spatter. I unbutton and take the coat off her, throwing it onto the back seat, as well. Then, I pull off my own jacket and manage to get Asya's arms into the sleeves, zipping her into its warmth. She doesn't say anything while I get her dressed. Her eyes seem vacant as she stares in front of her. I don't think she's even aware of me.

I shouldn't have let her do this. When she took the gun and turned toward the son of a bitch, I was certain she'd change her mind. I don't think the sound of a gunshot has ever shaken me this much.

"Mishka," I prompt her as I wipe the blood off her hand on the front of my hoodie. "Please say something."

Asya just blinks. Her eyes remain unfocused.

A small white flake lands on her cheek. Another one follows. I look up at the sky. It's snowing. I quickly grab the hood of the jacket and pull it over her head. "Let's go home, baby."

By the time I park the car in front of my building, the light snow has turned into a full-blown blizzard. Asya spent the entire two-hour drive curled up on the passenger seat with her face pressed to my shoulder.

"We're here," I say.

She nods and straightens up, but keeps her eyes closed. I exit the car and walk around the front. However, when I open the passenger door, Asya makes no attempt to move.

"Let's get you inside." I bend and scoop her into my arms.

The wind blows in my face, sending snow into my eyes as I carry her toward the building's entrance. The parking lot is barely forty feet away, but by the time we reach the doors, we're both covered in flurries.

As soon as we get inside the apartment, I set Asya down and remove her jacket. I take off my hoodie next. It's black, like the jacket, and the snow hasn't had a chance to melt off it, yet. I throw the hoodie behind me and crouch to unlace her boots. I need to call the doc's psychologist friend again and ask what to do. I can't tell her that I let Asya kill a man, but I need some kind of advice. What if she regresses? Her silence is freaking me out.

As I'm untying Asya's other boot, I feel her hands in my hair. Slowly, I look up and find her watching me with a strange look in her eyes.

"I never should have given you that gun," I whisper. "I'm so sorry, baby."

Asya cocks her head to the side and glides her hands down my neck and further, to the center of my back. Grabbing handfuls of material with her fingers, she pulls the T-shirt over my head and then starts unbuttoning her shirt. I regard her as she removes it and her bra and starts on her jeans. I'm still crouching in front of her as she pushes the discarded clothes to the side and stands bare before me.

Taking my hand in hers, she pulls me up and unbuttons my jeans. I can't take my eyes off her while she removes my shoes and the rest of my clothes, leaving us both naked in front of each other.

"Asya, baby?" As I reach out to caress her face, she jumps on me. I barely catch her in time, managing to grab a hold under her thighs. Her arms lock around my neck, legs wrap my waist as she dips her head until her lips touch the shell of my ear.

"Yes, Pashenka?" she whispers.

I suck in a breath. No one has ever called me that. The pakhan and a few others use my full name, but the rest call me Pasha—the Russian short variant for Pavel. But no one has ever used a diminutive name. In Russia, those are usually reserved for someone's closest family members and spouses.

"How do you know about that endearment?" I ask.

"I found a website about Russian names," she says and places a kiss on the side of my neck. "It mentioned that it's a very personal and affectionate name, and it's best to ask for permission before using it." She trails her mouth to the side of my jaw. "Do I have your permission to use it?"

"Yes," I whisper.

Her lips reach mine and hover just a breath away. "I want you to fuck me, Pashenka."

My cock swells upon hearing her say it. Squeezing her thighs, I turn around, pinning her to the front door. I can feel her dripping pussy against my abs, and it takes all my restraint not to bury my dick inside her. Asya bites my bottom lip, and my control snaps. Positioning her above my rock-hard cock, I start lowering her, inhaling her trembling breath as I fill her up. She moans into my lips, then squeezes my hair when I pull out.

"Harder." Her soft whimper transforms into a scream when I slam back inside.

As I drive into her pussy, I can feel her warmth, and it feels like coming home. I don't think I really knew what that phrase meant before meeting Asya. But this—her body pressed to mine, her hands in my hair, and her lips crushed against my mouth—it finally feels like home. She is my home. Squeezing her thighs, I thrust hard, wanting to imprint myself on her. To mark her as mine in some way.

"Harder." She moans and sinks her teeth into my shoulder.

I've long since lost the ability for rational thought. Purely on instinct, I turn around and carry her across the room to the dining table. Ignoring the neat stacks of financial documents I labored over yesterday which are now lining the tabletop, I lower Asya directly on one of the contracts. She's so wet that the paper under her ass gets instantly saturated.

"Lie down, baby." I grab her behind her knees and pull her closer, placing her feet at the edge of the table. She watches me through her spread legs, a tiny smirk lighting up her face.

"I'm waiting," she says.

I smile and take a step closer, letting just the tip of my cock find its home, and press my thumb over her clit. She sucks in a breath. I rub small circles on her nub, teasing her, then slowly push further in as I increase the pressure with my thumb. Before I'm even fully inside, her body starts trembling.

My cock hurts because of how hard it is, but I keep up my slow movements, watching her body arch off the table and reveling in each sound of pleasure she makes. With one last circle on her clit, I take her ankles and slowly straighten her legs to a perfect V. I pound into her, narrowing and widening her legs with every thrust and retreat.

"Harder!" she yells.

I rest her calves on my shoulders, press her knees together, and slam back inside. She orgasms, screaming out her pleasure while tremors shake her body. I can feel her pussy spasm around my cock, and it sends a jolt up my spine. I roar and explode into her.

I stroke the length of Asya's hair, then leisurely run my palm up and down her back. She's been sleeping on top of me for two hours now. I should try getting some sleep, too. I spent the previous night chasing and, once I caught him, beating the shit out of the motherfucker who hurt my girl. But I can't sleep. I keep thinking about Asya as she pulled that trigger.

It feels as if a countdown has begun with that bullet. The man who tore apart her life is gone. Roman assured me that the rest of the organization will be dealt with, so I'm sure they will all be dead by this time tomorrow.

I look down at Asya's face resting on the center of my chest. She usually tosses and turns in her sleep, but she hasn't moved a muscle since falling asleep earlier. I tug on the blanket at her hips and cover her fully.

How much time do we have left? She's been doing much

better these past few weeks, and I very rarely need to help her with decisions anymore. Men in suits still make her uncomfortable, but she's come a long way toward overcoming that, too. The nightmares have stopped, and the only thing that still distresses her is snow. I'm so fucking proud of her.

As good as her progress is, it fuels the utter panic rising within me. Will today be the day she'll tell me it's time for her to leave? Or will it be tomorrow? It's been weeks since I stopped urging her to contact her brother. I convinced myself that I did it to give her time and space to heal, but I've been lying to myself. I did it because I want her to stay. Forever.

As I watch her sleeping form, her presence lessens the gaping hole inside my chest, but the sound of a ticking clock echoes through my mind. Counting down the days, or maybe mere hours, I have left with her.

Tick. Tock.
Tick. Tock.

CHAPTER
eighteen

"**A**re you sure, Asya?" I ask as I hold the car door open for her.

"Nope." She takes my hand and exits the car "But I need to do it anyway."

"Okay, baby."

With Asya's hand clasped in mine, I head toward the back entrance of Ural. I still don't think it's a good idea to come to the club during the hours it's open to the public. It's not the same as going to the mall. Here, there will be more people in a smaller space, all crammed together. And since Ural is a more upscale place, most of the clubgoers will be wearing classy clothes, including suits on men. I know she needs to face her fears, but I don't like the idea of her getting stressed for any reason. I want to shield her from harm. But Asya has been insisting for two weeks, so I finally caved.

We leave our jackets at the coat check and enter the main space. There are already more than a hundred people inside. Asya wraps her arm around my forearm and leans into my side, but she doesn't falter as we head around the dance floor toward the opposite corner, bringing us near the stairs that lead to the upper level. I told the staff to remove the tables from that spot. We're halfway to our destination when a man waves at me from one of the VIP booths and then heads in our direction. Damian Rossi. The Chicago don's brother. He navigates through the crowd and meets us near the stairway.

"Pavel, I've been looking for you. How does renting this place for a night work?" He grins and looks over at Asya, offering her his hand. "I'm Damian."

"Hi," she says quietly but doesn't make a move to shake his hand.

I'm barely containing my urge to tell the Italian to go to hell, but Asya seems fine. I don't want her to think I doubt her ability to deal with the situation. She said she can handle it and, unless I notice distress, I won't interfere.

"Rentals are limited to the Bratva members only," I say. "What's the occasion?"

"Oh, nothing special. Some friends and I would like to throw a party, and we're looking for a venue." He shrugs, then turns back at Asya and his smile widens. "Would you like to come, *bellissima*? I didn't get your name."

Asya's hold on my forearm tightens.

"Leave, Damian," I say in a curt tone.

"What? I was just—"

I grab the front of his shirt and shove my face in his. "Turn around and leave. Right fucking now." I snarl through my teeth.

He blinks at me in confusion and raises his hands. "Okay, man. No need for a spat, especially in front of a lady."

I let go of his shirt and watch as he walks back to his booth.

"Do you want to leave?" I look down at Asya.

"I'm okay." She offers me a small smile. "Let's stay for a bit."

When we reach my intended spot, I lean against the wall and pull Asya to stand between my legs with her back pressed to my chest. She's wearing jeans and a simple sleeveless top with a high neckline. The fabric is soft lightweight wool and it's in the same shade of brown as her hair.

"All good?" I ask as I wrap my arms around her waist.

"Yeah."

We stand in silence and people watch for about ten minutes. She seems relaxed at first, but then leans more against me. Her hands come up to cover mine, squeezing my fingers.

I dip my head until my chin lands on her shoulder. "Talk to me."

"I'm okay. Just a little uneasy. There are a lot of people."

"Want to leave?"

She seems to be undecided for a few moments but then shakes her head. "Not yet. It's a bit unnerving, but I can handle it. I want to experience this a bit longer."

I grit my teeth. I don't want her around anything that makes her uncomfortable. And I certainly don't like the fact that she's feeling unsettled. If she wants to stay, okay. But it'll be under my new conditions. I spin her around, grab her under her thighs, and lift her.

She yelps in surprise and locks her feet behind my back. "Pasha?"

I face the wall, bracing her on it and letting her see the dance floor.

"Now you can keep checking things out," I bite out.

Asya arches her eyebrows at me and smiles. "I like the new view even better." She leans forward and presses her lips to mine. "So much better."

I nip her lower lip. Asya sucks in a breath and tightens her legs around me. My cock swells. I can feel the heat of her pussy next to my hard length, and my dick hardens even more when she grabs at the back of my neck and sinks her teeth into my chin.

"Maybe we could head home after all," she says into my mouth. "What do you say, Pashenka?"

I don't reply, just turn around and carry her toward the exit.

Asya

I almost trip trying to get out of my pants without letting go of Pasha's neck. My shoes and top are somewhere in the living room, along with his jeans and T-shirt. I'm not sure, but I think our jackets may be in the hallway in front of the elevator. Finally free of my jeans, I walk backward to the bed, trying to unclasp my bra with one hand. Pasha slips off his boxer briefs, grabs me around the waist, and throws us onto the bed. I end up sprawled on top of his chest.

"I want us to try something," I say and nip at his chin. "I saw it online."

"What?"

"Umm . . . it's a position." I smile sheepishly and scrape my teeth over my lower lip.

Pasha lifts an eyebrow. "Oh? Something specific?"

His hands slide down my back and squeeze my ass. In his hands, every inch of my skin feels as if it's been zapped by a live wire. I still find it hard to believe how much I enjoy him touching me. Kissing me. Making love to me. I was afraid, at first, that I might freak out at some point, forgetting who he is, and flinch at his touch. The idea that it may happen was constantly present in my mind for a while. I loathed the possibility of unintentionally hurting him if I involuntarily recoiled, making him think he did something wrong. I'm not afraid of that anymore. Both my body and my mind recognize him, no matter what's going on. Even when he's rough. Even when he pushes me against the wall and takes me from behind. There's not a speck of fear. Just mind-blowing pleasure.

"Yes." I smirk and feel the heat in my cheeks.

Pasha moves his hands up my back, then takes my face between my palms, pulling me in for a kiss. "Turn around."

"You know what I have in mind?"

"Based on how red your face is, I'm pretty sure I do." He bites at my lip. "Come on, give me your pretty pussy."

I flip and face his cock, leaving my pussy exposed to his mouth. Pasha grabs at my butt cheeks, pulling me closer, and buries his face between my legs. His tongue circles my entrance, then slides inside, making me gasp. As I reach for his cock, my hands are trembling from the overwhelming sensations. I squeeze his hard length and take the tip into my mouth. Pasha changes his tempo—slow licks and kisses turn frenzied—eating my pussy as if it's dessert. The combined feeling of his tongue on my pussy and his cock in my mouth isn't comparable to anything I've ever experienced before.

He adds his fingers and then pinches my clit, and I come all over his face.

It takes me a few moments to recover from the high, and then I take him deeper into my throat as he keeps lapping up my juices. His breathing is labored. I can tell he's close. I leisurely ease my mouth off his hard length and turn around to face him. Locking my eyes with Pasha's, I position myself over his straining cock and slowly lower myself, marveling at the feel of him filling me up. Pasha's hand shoots up, grabbing me behind my neck, and stays there as I rock my hips while he stares into my eyes, unblinking. Strained breaths leave his lips, and the muscles on his chest are taut under my palms, but it's the look on his face that holds my attention. His jaw is clenched, his lips flattened. It seems like he wants to say something, but he's holding back.

"What's wrong, Pashenka?" I ask as I lift my ass, then drop back down, gasping as his cock drives deep into me.

His hold on my neck tightens, but he doesn't utter a word. Just slams into me from below so hard that my mind goes blank. The next moment, I find myself on my back with Pasha's body over mine. He continues to grip my neck while thrusting so fast that my body shakes and I can barely get enough air into my lungs. I love when he lets go of his steely self-control and fucks me with all his power. There's nothing better than having him screw me until we come at the same time. It makes me feel strong, fearless, and happier than I've ever been. I grab his arms and shout out his name as another orgasm erupts.

CHAPTER
nineTeen

⊷•⊶•⊷ 🔫 Pavel 🔫 ⊷•⊶•⊷

SLOW, EMOTIONAL NOTES DRIFT IN FROM THE LIVING room. I open my eyes and stare at the ceiling. A little while ago she played "Für Elise." I don't know the name of this particular melody, though, and I rarely ask because I prefer when Asya tells me on her own. Her music is very personal to her, so the fact she shares something she feels this intimate about, without me asking for it, strikes a deep chord in my soul. Early on, I got used to not asking for things in my life, and it became a habit. Why ask for things when the answer will almost always be no? Yes, there's a possibility for a different outcome, but I guess I prefer not asking over dealing with disappointment.

My first few years in foster care, I kept asking the same three questions. *Did my mother call? Did anyone call looking for me? Will my mother come back?* The answer was always no. Then, the questions changed. *Do I have any other family? Will another family pick me like some of the other kids?* Like that trou-blemaker, the boy who kept fighting with the other boys at one of the homes I lived at. I don't remember his name. Was it Kane? Or maybe Kai? Two of the other foster kids ended up in the emergency room when they teased him about his long hair. The crazy fucker bit off a chunk of one's ear and stabbed a fork into the other's neck. That boy disappeared after that, and we all thought he ended up in juvie or a mental institution. But a few months later I overheard the social workers saying he was adopted. So, I resumed pestering the foster parents and the social workers day after day, asking if someone would adopt me, too. I asked and asked until my foster dad got fed up with it and yelled into my face to stop asking idiotic questions. I followed his advice.

Is it my fear of rejection that makes it so hard for me to ask Asya to stay with me? Last night, I almost did. I wanted to ask her so much that I barely managed to stop the words from exploding out of my mouth. She might have said yes. I know she likes spending time with me. I think she even likes me, but remaining with me would mean not returning to her family. Does she like me enough to choose me over them?

The melody in the living room changes. I know this one. It's the piano version of the *Game of Thrones* intro. Asya loves that one. I roll out of bed, intending on dragging her back to bed, just as my phone rings on the nightstand. Roman's name lights up the screen.

"Pakhan?" I ask when I answer the call.

"I need to talk with you, Pavel."

"All right." I nod and sit on the bed.

"In person," he adds in an ominous voice. "I'll expect you at the mansion in an hour."

The line disconnects.

I step inside the pakhan's office and find him seated behind his desk. Mikhail and Sergei are there, too, lounging in the recliners by the bookshelf.

"Pakhan." I close the door behind me and head toward his desk. "Is something wrong at the clubs?"

"Not exactly," he says. "Tell me, Pavel, is there anything I need to know? Something you forgot to mention, maybe?"

"About what?"

He tilts his head to the side, regarding me. "Does the name DeVille sound familiar to you?"

A chill runs down my spine.

Roman smiles. It's not a nice smile. "I see it does." He leans forward and hits the desk with his palm. "What the fuck were you thinking, hiding Arturo DeVille's sister at your place?"

It takes me a few moments to recover. How the fuck did he find out?

"She doesn't want anyone to know. Her brother included," I say through my teeth. "When she's ready, she'll call him."

"I don't give a fuck what she wants!" Roman snarls. "Her brother has been searching for her for months, thinking she's dead! Can you at least imagine what it's been like for him? His baby sister, gone, not knowing if she's dead or alive?"

I fist my hands and grind my teeth. "Asya doesn't want to call him, Roman."

"Do you know she has a sister, Pavel?" Roman continues. "A sister who spent two weeks in the hospital after she swallowed a bottle of sleeping pills because she believed it was her fault that Asya went missing?"

"Shit." I close my eyes. "Is she okay? Her sister?"

"She's okay."

"How do you know all this?" I ask and look at him.

"When Asya went missing, Ajello sent a message to all Cosa Nostra Families, demanding they report it if anyone sees her. He sent her photo." The pakhan sighs. "Damian Rossi saw you two at Ural last night. Arturo was at my door at six this morning."

I grab the back of the chair in front of me, gripping it hard enough to make my knuckles turn white. "Did you tell him where she is?"

Roman throws a look toward where Mikhail and Sergei are sitting. "He's currently on his way to your place, Pavel."

I stare at him while fear worse than any I've ever experienced spreads from the pit of my stomach. He is going to take her away. I turn on my heel, ready to rush out of the office and head home, only to find Sergei blocking my exit.

"Move!" I snarl and lunge at him, but two arms grab me from behind.

"Pasha. Calm down," Mikhail says, restraining me.

I thrust my head back, headbutting his forehead. Mikhail's hold falters and I use the opportunity and lunge at Sergei. He gets my head with his fist, but I throw my elbow into his stomach. I dodge, avoiding his next punch, and take a swing at his face just as Mikhail rushes me from behind, pinning me against the wall beside the door.

"You can't fucking keep a person from their family!" he roars next to my ear and bangs my head against the wall.

"He'll take her away!"

185

"He can't take her away if she doesn't want to go," Mikhail says. "But if she wants to, you don't have the right to make her stay."

"I know." I close my eyes and slump against the wall, defeated.

"Let him go, Mikhail. You can leave," Roman says from somewhere behind me. "You, too, Sergei."

I hear the door opening and retreating steps, but I don't move. My forehead rests on the cool surface. I'm slowly going numb.

"Pavel, look at me."

I open my eyes and tilt my head to the side. Roman is standing next to me, leaning on his cane.

"You need to let her go. If you don't, neither you nor her will know if she's with you because she loves you. Or if it's because she's afraid to leave."

"You don't understand," I say. "I've never had any-one, Roman. Until her. I can't imagine my life without her anymore."

"She needs to go see her sister. She needs her family. And her family needs her. But she will return."

I look at the wall again. "She won't. If she leaves, she won't be back."

"Why are you so certain?"

"Because she doesn't need me now, Roman. She needed me before. Not anymore."

"Do you want her to stay with you just because she needs you? You deserve better than that. Both of you do."

"I know." I bang my forehead on that goddamned wall as if it'll help stifle the terror raging inside me.

"Go home. Talk to her. Talk to Arturo, he deserves an

explanation." Roman places his hand on my shoulder and squeezes. "Take a few days off if you need to. And please stop banging your thick head against my wall. You'll break the fucking thing."

"My head?" I ask.

"The wall, Pavel. If your skull didn't crack during all those years of fighting, it certainly won't now."

I snort and shake my head.

Asya

There is a knock on the door.

My fingers still on the piano keys. Pasha never knocks. He always rings the bell. It must be a neighbor wanting to ask me not to play so loud. I cross the living room and open the door. When my eyes land on the man standing on the other side, I quickly take a step back.

"Dear God," my brother chokes out and pulls me into a bear hug, squeezing me so hard that it's impossible to move a muscle.

I try to gulp a deep breath, but no air seems to enter my lungs. Another try. Arturo eases his hold and looks down at me with a slightly crazed look in his eyes. And then, he's squishing me to his body again. My arms are shaking as I embrace him and press my cheek to his chest.

"I thought you were dead," he says into my hair. "I thought someone took you, and I've been waiting for someone to call and ask for a ransom. The call never came."

"I'm sorry," I mumble, tears gathering in the corners of

my eyes. It's hard to believe he's here after all this time. And it feels good. "I'm so sorry, Arturo."

"Why, Asya? Why not let us know that you're okay?" He cups my face between his palms and tilts my head up. "Where have you been all this time?"

I watch my brother while worry ignites a foreboding feeling in the pit of my stomach, spreading the heated pulses of dread up my chest.

"We found your purse and glasses behind that bar. And blood. What happened?"

I open my mouth, but no words leave my lips.

"Jesus fuck, Asya, say something, damn it!"

"I was raped!" I yell into his face.

All color leaves Arturo's face. He blinks. His hands on my cheeks start shaking. I wrap my arms around his back and bury my face into his chest.

And then I talk, but I don't tell him everything.

When I'm done, Arturo lowers himself to his knees in front of me, still holding me in his embrace. I thread my fingers in his hair and lean my cheek on top of his head, listening to him as he mumbles how he's going to crucify the son of a bitch who hurt me, then how much he loves me.

"I love you, too, Arturo," I whisper.

And that's why I haven't told him the whole story. I skipped the worst part. It's better like this.

"We need to call Sienna," Arturo murmurs. "I didn't want to tell her anything until I was sure. In case . . . in case it wasn't you, I couldn't risk her doing something stupid again."

"What do you mean?"

He shakes his head and holds me harder.

"What did she do, Arturo?"

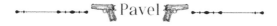

Pavel

The first thing I notice when I step inside the apartment is a dark-haired man sitting on the sofa in my living room. He's looking at the floor between his feet, elbows leaning on his knees as his hands grip his hair.

"Where's Asya?" I ask.

"Taking a shower. Preparing to leave," he says, still looking at the floor.

"She told you everything?"

"Yes. I also know she's been here this whole time."

I cross the living room and take a seat on the recliner to his left. "I need to give you some pointers on Asya."

His head snaps up, and two dark brown eyes, the same shade as Asya's, pin me with a stare full of hatred. "I don't need you to give me fucking pointers on my sister. I raised her since she was five."

I ignore his hostility. "She still has problems making some decisions. We worked out almost everything, but she may need help from time to time. Try not to give her specific direction, but rather steer her toward it."

He stares at me in silence.

"No daisies. Not flowers, and nothing else, either, like curtains or whatnot with pictures of them," I continue. "She's not triggered by suits anymore, but men's ties can still distress her. If you're in public, and the place is crowded with unfamiliar men wearing suits, you need to hold her hand."

He looks down at himself, focusing on his silk gray tie,

then lifts his head and passes his eyes over my T-shirt and jeans. When he moves his gaze up and our eyes meet, I see the loathing there.

"Jesus fuck!" he barks. "You're in love with her."

I don't look away as I reply, "Yes."

"She's eighteen, for God's sake! You are too old for her. Asya needs someone her age. And definitely not an ex-convict."

"You checked me out?"

"Of course I checked you out. I wanted to know the man who was keeping my sister from me. I even dug up videos of some of your fights."

"Well, I hope they were entertaining."

Arturo leans forward and pins me with his gaze. "You tried to steal my baby sister! An abused, hurt girl. You kept her from her family, even though you knew she needed us," he spits out. "I don't know what kind of sick fantasy you created, playing house with a teenager, and I don't care. I won't let you get near her again! Ever! My sister deserves better."

"I know." I rise and head to the stand by the front door where I keep some pens and paper. "I'll give you my number. Call me if you need any help."

I walk back and drop the paper on the coffee table in front of Arturo, then head toward the front door. "I'll come back in two hours. Will you be gone by then?"

"No goodbye?" he raises his eyebrows.

"No," I say.

"Good."

I nod and leave the apartment.

I'm sitting in my car two streets down from my building when my phone rings. "Moonlight Sonata" surrounds me. I lean my head back and watch the cars passing down the street. The ringing stops but immediately starts again. I let it run its course, the sound reverberating through the small space. I could have silenced it. Every fucking tone feels like a knife to my chest, but I didn't. The phone rings four more times, and I let it ring through every fucking time.

A message arrives. I take the phone off the dash and look at the screen. It's a voice mail. I hit play.

"Pasha? What's going on? Arturo said that you came home and left? Did something happen?" Rustling in the background. "We're heading to the airport. I need to go see Sienna. She . . ." Sniffing. "My sister tried to kill herself. She thought what happened to me was her fault. I'll stay with her for a few days and then I'm coming back. I'll call you when I get there" Her voice sounded shaky. Was she crying?

The message ends. I hit play again. And again.

It's almost midnight. I'm lying on the couch, gripping the phone as it continues to ring in my hand. I want to swipe that green button and take the call so much; it's making me crazy. I don't. My mind keeps replaying that one sentence Asya's brother said.

You kept her from her family, even though you knew she needed us.

He was right. I should have contacted him to let him know she was safe. If I explained the situation, he might have agreed to wait until Asya was ready to face him. But I was too selfish and too fucking terrified that he would take her away from me. I could no longer imagine my life without her. The possibility of her leaving scared the fuck out of me and I was ready to do whatever was needed to make sure she stayed. So, I kept my promise to her and remained silent, a self-preserving son of a bitch. I became her fucking demon. No one deserves to be with such a person, especially not Asya.

I've always believed I would be able to measure love by how much I would want to be with a person. Deciding to be with someone for the rest of my life seemed like the pinnacle of love. Wrong. I understand things much better now. Knowing that Asya, the woman I love, will be better off without me, I had to let her go. Even though it hurts. Even when it's shredding me on the inside. Maybe, if I loved Asya a little less, I would have found a way to keep her with me. I love her too much to do that to her, though, so I've let her go.

I should have answered the call. Said goodbye, at least. But I couldn't. Hearing her say she'll come back, but knowing that she won't, I couldn't risk speaking to her. I would have done something stupid, like make her promise she'll return to me.

My eyes land on the piano near the living room window. Why didn't she take the damn thing with her? I get up off the sofa and head into the kitchen to grab the toolbox from where I keep it under the sink. When I come back to the living room, I'm holding a hammer in my hand. Walking to the instrument, I intend to smash the thing until there is nothing left of it, but instead, I end up staring at the keys for an hour. Asya loves this piano. The hammer falls from my hand, hitting the polished floor with a loud thud. I can't make myself destroy something that brought her joy.

My phone rings. I grab it and throw the fucking thing across the room.

It's better like this for her. She won't feel obliged to call me out of some misplaced sense of gratitude or whatever. It might be hard for her to adjust for the first few days at home, but she has her family now. Friends, too. Soon enough, she'll forget all about me and continue with her life. Maybe I'll do the same.

The phone rings again. It rings two more times that night.

It keeps ringing at least ten times every day for the following five days.

On the sixth day, it rings only once, and then the calls stop.

CHAPTER
Twenty

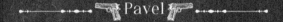

Pavel

Three weeks later

I PARK MY CAR A BLOCK AWAY FROM ASYA'S HOME AND head up the street.

Flying in would have been much easier. Instead, I drove thirteen hours, hoping I'd change my mind along the way and turn around. I stopped three times and almost convinced myself to do exactly that, but when I got back on the road, I just continued heading east. The need to see her again is an obsession, the only thing I've thought about for days. Just one quick glimpse, and I'll be gone.

Something wet lands on my cheek, so I peer at the night sky. It's snowing. My chest tightens at the sight of the white flakes as they fall on my face. My mishka doesn't like snow. It's the one thing we weren't able to overcome.

I promised myself that I won't keep hoping for her return. I knew she wouldn't, not after all the calls I didn't take and the messages I left unanswered. Yet, I still hoped.

Last week, feeling more miserable than ever, I dug out the box with my tattoo kit from the back of the closet. Why I've kept that thing, I don't have a clue. I stopped adding tats more than a decade ago. That night, though, I sat down at my dining table, in my empty apartment, and got working on new ink. Since there weren't any free spots on my torso or my arms, I did it on the back of my hand. When Kostya saw me the following day, he asked if it was one of those temporary things because I'd never tattooed a part of my body that was visible before. I told him what I thought of his opinion with my freshly inked knuckles.

I can see only the upper part of the house at the top of the street. Most of it is hidden behind the high gated fence and greenery, but it matches the description Dimitri was able to find. Asya's home.

I'm still observing the house, trying to spot the light in one of the windows, when a flashy car rounds the corner and parks right in front of the gate. There's a streetlight close by, so I step back into the shadow of a tree. The man who gets out of the driver's side is young, probably in his early twenties. He's smiling, obviously in a great mood. He opens the passenger door, and a woman takes his hand and steps out. She's wearing a white coat, unbuttoned, revealing a blood-red dress underneath. It's snowing harder now, and snowflakes stick to the dress's feathered skirt. The man grabs her around the waist, crashing her into his body. The woman laughs.

I know that laugh. I want to turn away and leave, but I can't take my eyes off the woman as she tilts her head and kisses the man. It's not a friendly kiss, but a passionate one. The man's hand glides up her back.

The gate slides to the side, and the woman untangles

herself from the embrace. A moment before she disappears through the gate, I catch a glimpse of her face. She's cut her hair. It's shoulder-length now, but there is no doubt.

It's my Asya.

Something breaks inside my chest. I'm pretty sure it's my heart.

The gate closes and the car leaves, but I keep standing in the shadows, staring at the house beyond the fence.

She's okay. I'm not sure if the man I saw is just a date or a boyfriend, but it doesn't really matter. She's moved on. I expected her to, but seeing it hurts so fucking much. She deserves to be happy, though. And I'm glad she is.

I turn around and head back to my car, snow crunching under the soles of my shoes. I couldn't sleep in my own bed after she left, so I spent the first few nights on the couch, then moved into one of the empty bedrooms.

But I can't do it anymore. I can't be in that place or pretend to live my old life.

When I'm inside my car, I call Roman.

"Pavel?" comes his voice from the other side.

I look at the house up the street one last time.

"I quit," I say and cut the connection.

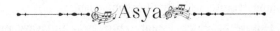

Asya

I put down the phone and watch my sister take off her heels and head into the closet.

"That thing is awful," I say.

"What?" Sienna turns around and juts her hip. "This is from the newest collection."

It always amazes me how two people can look identical on the outside but have widely different personalities and tastes.

"It has fucking feathers, Sienna. How do you even wash it?"

"Dry cleaning," she says and unzips the red monstrosity. "When are you planning on getting out of the house? We can go hiking in the Catskills."

"Hiking?" I arch my eyebrows. The highest my sister has ever climbed was onto a stool to get the old hairdryer off the shelf when her regular one died.

"What? It could be fun."

I shake my head and look back down at my phone. "I'm not in the mood."

Sienna stops fumbling with her dress and plops onto the bed beside me. "You need to forget that guy, Asya. He doesn't want anything to do with you. You should have clued in already."

"You don't know that."

"You've phoned him over fifty times! I checked your call history," she says and grabs my phone. "Please don't tell me you called him again."

"Give that back!" I jump at her, trying to get my cell. "Sienna!"

"You did! I can't believe you."

"I haven't called him." I take my phone from her. "I was looking at some photos."

"What photos?"

I shrug.

"You never told me you had a photo of him!" Sienna widens her eyes at me. "Let me see! Please? Please? Please?"

I unlock my phone and reluctantly pass it to her. She grabs it with a squeal and starts going through the folders.

"Oh, I can't wait to . . . holy fuck, Asya! Is this him?"

I glance at the screen, at the photo of Pasha I secretly took one morning while he was still sleeping. He's on his back with his arm thrown over his face. The blanket is bunched up around his waist, leaving his tattooed broad chest fully on display.

"Yeah." I nod.

Sienna flips to the next image. That one's a little blurry, taken the day he gave me the phone. I was trying out the camera with a selfie but moved my hand too fast. In the photo, I'm leaning against Pasha's chest and gazing at the camera. He has his arm wrapped around my waist and is looking down at me.

"I still don't understand what happened," I say, looking at the screen. "Why did he shut me out? Did I do something? Did he decide he can't deal with my issues anymore?"

"Asya, stop." Sienna takes my hand. "You didn't do anything wrong. You hear me? He doesn't deserve you, not after how he acted."

"I miss him so much," I whisper and look back down at the phone. I wish I took more photos of him.

"It'll get easier. You'll meet a guy, fall in love, and forget all about the Russian." She wraps her arm around me and pulls me into a hug. "When you're ready, we'll go out together and find the most handsome, sweet guy for you. Okay?"

A heavy feeling settles over me, and I close my eyes. I don't want a sweet, handsome guy. I want Pasha. Just the thought of any other man touching me makes me sick to my stomach. Acid rises up my throat, so I fan my face, hoping the nausea will pass. It doesn't. It only gets worse. I jump off the bed and dash to the bathroom, barely managing to reach the toilet in time. Sienna runs in after me and lifts my hair away from my face as I empty the contents of my stomach. When I'm done, I slump to the floor next to the toilet and stare at the ceiling.

"I can't even think about other men without vomiting, Sienna," I whisper.

CHAPTER
twenty-one

Asya

One month later

MY PHONE RINGS AS I'M REARRANGING MY closet for the third time this week. I found that folding stuff helps me keep my mind thought-free. Funny thing, I've also started sorting my clothes by color.

I reach for the cell and see that it's an unknown caller. Only a couple of people have this number because I'm still using the phone Pasha gave me. Somewhere deep inside, I'm still hopeful he'll call, but it's been nearly two months.

"Yes?"

"Asya?" a vaguely familiar male voice asks. "Can you please put that piece of shit on the line? He's been ignoring my calls for weeks, and I have a clusterfuck on my hands at Ural."

I raise my eyebrows. "Kostya?"

"Of course, it's me, sweetheart. Who else has such a sexy voice? Oh fuck, please don't tell him I called you sweetheart."

"Tell who?"

"Pasha, of course. Can you please put him on? It's taken me two days to crack the password on his email account to find your number. Things here are getting disastrous."

Why would Kostya think Pasha's with me? I swallow the lump that's suddenly formed in my throat and close my eyes. "He's not here."

"Please tell him to call me when he—"

"He is not here, Kostya. I haven't seen him since I left Chicago," I choke out.

"What? He's not with you? Did he call you recently?"

"No. I've called him, but he never answered," I say. "What's going on?"

For a moment, there's nothing but silence before Kostya replies. "Pasha quit a month ago."

"Quit? You can't just quit the Bratva. Petrov is going to hunt him down and kill him!"

"Roman won't kill him, but I don't think Pasha cares." A Russian curse comes from the other side, then a sound of something breaking. "No one knows where he is. He took my calls the first week, but then nothing. He hasn't been at his apartment, so I hoped he was with you."

Dread pools in my stomach. "Has he disappeared before?"

"Pavel?" he laughs, but it sounds forced. "He hasn't taken a single day off since he joined the Bratva. Well, before you, I mean."

"Where is he, then?" I mean to ask the question calmly, but I end up sounding like I'm yelling because my voice is higher than normal and trembling.

"I have no idea, Asya."

I pace the room, trying to calm down, but my chest is tight and my heart is racing. I have a bad feeling that something truly awful is about to happen. "I need you to call me the moment you hear from him. Please."

"Sure, sweetheart. I'll make a few calls to see if anyone's seen or heard from him and then I'll let you know."

When we end the call, I walk to the window overlooking the garden and stare at nothing in particular. I promised myself I wouldn't call him ever again. If he wants to talk, he can call me.

I look down at my phone and press the speed dial number. It rings. And rings. Closing my eyes, I lean my forehead against the window and keep listening to the ringing sound until it disconnects without rolling over to voice mail. I call again. And again. After the fourth try, a message arrives. I'm afraid of what it may say, so I stare at his name for at least ten minutes before I gather the courage and open it.

23:15 Pasha: Stop calling, mishka. Please.

"Fuck you!" I yell at the screen and throw the phone on the bed. And then I cry.

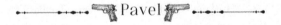

Pavel

The familiar sounds of cheering and yelling surround me. Just as the stench of sweat mixed with the faint smell of mold does, too. Laughter rings out and then more hollers. I lean my back on the concrete wall and stare at the phone in my hand and the text I just sent.

She called. Staring at her name on the screen, not

answering those calls, was the hardest fucking thing I've ever done. If she continued calling, I would have probably caved.

I check the call log. There're hundreds of missed calls over the last few weeks. At least fifty are from Kostya, but there are dozens from Roman, and Mikhail, too. The rest of the guys have been calling, as well. Even Sergei. I never answered. I didn't feel like talking. What was there to say, anyway?

I press my thumb over Asya's name at the top of the list, swipe to the side and delete the entry. Then, I flip back to the sent message and delete that, as well. Seeing her name hurts too much. I should clear her number, but it wouldn't do any good. I memorized it the moment I bought the phone for her.

A metal door on the other side of the room screeches as it opens, and a man enters. In his black suit and tie, he looks like a businessman. Well, considering the people who come to watch these fights and the amount of money that changes hands every night, they do need to keep it sleek.

"You're next," he says a moment before the bell chimes, followed by excited shouts. "Try not to incapacitate your opponent in the first round this time. The crowd likes to watch them struggle a bit."

I finish wrapping my hands, get up, and head toward the door while more cheers erupt from the direction of the fighting cage.

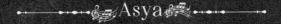

Asya

THE PHONE VIBRATES NEXT TO MY PILLOW. I SPRING up in bed and hit the button to take the call, then press the phone on my ear.

"Did you find him?" I whisper.

"Yes," Kostya says from the other end.

I close my eyes and breathe. Four fucking days have passed. "So, he's okay?"

"He is. In a way."

My eyes snap open. "What do you mean 'in a way?'"

Kostya sighs. "He's fighting again."

"What?"

"Yeah. I tried talking to him. It didn't go well. Roman called him, as well. He even went to his last match. Pasha doesn't want to come back."

"But . . . why? He told me he quit fighting ten years ago!"

"Pasha is a very closed-off guy, sweetheart. Who knows what's going on in that head of his?"

I bury my hand in my hair, squeezing it. "Are those matches dangerous?"

He doesn't reply.

"Are they, Kostya?" I scream into the phone.

"It's underground fighting, Asya. What do you expect?"

"I don't know! I've never been to a boxing match!"

"It's not a boxing match, sweetheart. Boxing has rules. These fights don't," he says in a grim tone as my phone pings with an incoming message. "I sent you the link to the club website and a password to access it. Search for 'Pavel Morozov fights' and see for yourself. But skip the last match."

"Why?" I choke out.

He takes a deep breath. "I know you like him, sweetie. Please, don't watch the newest video."

When Kostya ends the call, I open the message with the link and click on it. At first glance, the website looks like an ordinary gym promo site with images of exercise equipment and people stretching or lifting weights. In the upper right corner, I find a login button. I click on it and enter the ten-digit password Kostya sent with the link. A new window pops up and I immediately notice the chart. The first column shows names, and I spot Pasha's listed second from the top, just under another guy's name. Next to the names are rankings and number of wins. Pasha is currently ranked second. Below the standings chart is this month's schedule. I scroll to the bottom and note there is only one match left this month, set for tomorrow night. It's between Pasha and the guy ranked first. I scroll back up to see the number of wins. Next to Pasha's name is twelve. I glance at the number for the other competitor and my blood goes cold. It's fifty-four.

"Jesus fuck." I sink to the floor and lean my back to the

wall, then type "Pavel Morozov" into the search. A collection of videos pops up. The oldest one is dated a month ago. I hit play.

I'm not sure what I expected. Probably a fighting ring and some people standing around it. At least, that's how I imagined boxing matches to be like. What I'm seeing looks nothing like that. The video starts with the view from above, showing the inside of some abandoned factory or a warehouse. In the center, set on a raised platform, is an octagonal cage. Around the cage, men and a few women are seated on cushy chairs. All of them are impeccably dressed as if they came for a business meeting and not to watch a fighting match. Some even have bodyguards standing nearby.

A metal door across from the cage opens and two men enter. The camera zooms in on the fighters, and I almost don't recognize him. Pasha shaved his hair—all of it. But somehow, that's not the biggest change. His posture, the way he walks, and the grim expression on his face make him look as if he's someone else. He climbs into the cage and takes the spot on one side while his opponent heads for the opposite end. The referee signals for the start.

Pasha and his rival circle each other. He swipes at Pasha's side, but Pasha dodges and grabs the man's head, kneeing him in the face. Blood bursts from the guy's nose, and I look away from the screen. When I gather enough courage to look again, Pasha is standing over his opponent, pressing the fallen man's face to the floor. I've never watched a boxing match, but I had the impression those lasted for at least half an hour. This one is done in less than two minutes. The referee signals Pasha's victory and the video ends. I steel myself and click on the next recording.

It takes me almost an hour to watch the first ten videos. I have to pause and collect myself several times before continuing. So much violence. Blood. Broken bones. Each video is more violent than the previous one. It's killing me to watch my Pasha become so vicious. Bloodthirsty. I don't recognize this person as the man I spent three months with. What happened to him? Why is he doing this? There're two videos left, but I can't make myself watch them. It hurts too much.

Sometimes, I wish Arturo hadn't found me. I know it would have destroyed him and my sister. Sienna still blames herself, even though I've explained at least a hundred times that it was me who made the decision to remain at the bar that night. Still, sometimes when I can't sleep, which is often lately, I imagine what my life would be like if my brother hadn't come and I stayed in Chicago.

I still don't understand why Pasha pushed me away. I tried to think of a reason for his behavior, but I can't.

It's almost seven in the morning, but I can't sleep. Not after what I've just watched. I'll wait for Arturo and Sienna to wake up, then try playing the piano again. I haven't been able to complete a full melody since returning home. At least twice a day, I've gone to the ground floor and sat in front of the big black piano, staring at the keys. Most of the time, no music came, and I left it as quiet as it was when I arrived. Other times, when I actually tried to play, every note came out wrong.

I take my cardigan off the chair and leave my room, heading downstairs to grab some breakfast. As I'm passing Arturo's room, I overhear my name being mentioned, so I stop. He's talking with someone on the phone. I lean forward and press my ear to the door.

"She's not the same, Nino," my brother says. "I don't know what to do. She barely leaves her room."

There are a few moments of silence while he probably listens to what Nino is saying.

"No!" Arturo barks. "I'm not calling that son of a bitch. I told him what I thought about him and his attempt to keep Asya from us. Hiding my sister and not allowing her to contact us? What kind of sick bastard does that?"

What?! I grab the knob and throw open the door, heart pounding a rapid tattoo against my ribs. My brother stands by the bed with the phone pressed to his ear.

"What exactly did you tell Pasha, Arturo?" I shout.

"I'll call you later," he mumbles and throws the phone on the bed.

"What?" I yell.

"The truth," he says. "I told him the truth—that he kept you hidden to serve his own selfish needs. That he used a young, wounded girl and made her stay with him instead of returning her to her family. To her life. That he's a sick bastard. That's what I told him."

I stare at my brother, stunned at what I'm hearing, then take two steps until I'm right in front of him. "He saved my life, Arturo."

"Any normal person would have helped a woman in need. But they wouldn't have tried to hide her."

I close my eyes. When Arturo came to get me, I only told him about what Robert did. He thinks I spent the entire time with Pasha. I hoped it wouldn't come to this, that I wouldn't need to tell him what happened during those first two months or what those people did to me. What they made me do. I should have, but I didn't want to hurt him.

"Sit down, Arturo," I say, and when he does, I start talking. I tell him everything this time.

When I'm done, he's looking at me with red-rimmed eyes, hands gripping his hair while he's barely keeping himself on the edge of the bed. I don't think I've ever seen my brother cry, not even when we were told our parents had been killed.

"Why didn't you tell me?" he chokes out, then grabs me and engulfs me in a hug, crushing me against him. "Why, Asya? Why?" he whispers.

"I was in a very bad place when Pasha found me," I say into his neck. "Something had broken inside me, Arturo, and it felt as if I was trapped in a black hole with no way out. He saved me. And not only my life. He saved my soul, too. He helped me collect all my broken pieces and glued them back together."

"It should have been us," he says into my hair. "Sienna and I should have been the ones who helped you go through that."

"I couldn't make myself tell you. I didn't want to see you or Sienna. I would have rather died than told you."

"Why?"

"Because I wasn't ready. And because I love you and couldn't bear the thought of what it would do to you." I lift my head and take my brother's face in my palms. "I begged Pasha not to call you. I asked him to promise he wouldn't call you until I was ready. It wasn't him who kept me from you. I did that. It was my decision."

"I should have kept you safe," Arturo persists. "I will never forgive myself."

"Please don't do that. It's not your fault."

"I'm going to kill them all, Asya. Every single person who was in any way involved."

"Pasha and the Bratva already took care of them," I say, then tilt my chin up to whisper into his ear, "and I killed the guy who took me."

Arturo's body goes still. "You, personally?"

"Yes. After Pasha was done with him, I put a gun between the bastard's eyes and pulled the trigger." I smile. "It was the best fucking feeling ever."

"Good." He squeezes the back of my neck.

"I need to know what else you said to Pasha. He's been ignoring me, not taking my calls since I left."

Arturo grinds his teeth and looks away. "I told him that you deserve better, and he agreed."

I take a deep breath and close my eyes while pressure forms at the bridge of my nose. "You had no right," I say. "You had no right, Arturo. It's my life."

"You're eighteen, Asya. He's fifteen years older than you!"

"Yes. And I've gone through tough times most people don't ever experience," I bite out. "I think I've earned the right to make decisions for myself."

Yes, I still have problems picking what to wear or eat sometimes, but I don't have any doubts as far as Pasha is concerned.

"So, what happens now?" he asks. "Are you going back to him?"

"You will always be my big brother, Arturo. You know I love you unconditionally." I look into his eyes. "But I'm in love with Pasha. And I want to be with him."

"Are you sure you're in love with him? Maybe it's just a crush? Maybe—"

I raise my hand and put a finger over his lips to silence him.

"When Pasha found me, I was a wreck, Arturo. Both my soul and my mind . . . fractured. Pasha pieced me back together. And my heart yearns for him because he is the glue that keeps all my broken parts whole. Please, try to understand."

Arturo stares at me while grinding his jaw. "I'm going to drop by your place at least once a month. Unannounced. If I notice anything, even the smallest thing that will lead me to believe you're not happy, I'm going to kill that Russian and drag you back home."

"You won't have to." I smile., "I love him. I'll be okay, Arturo."

My brother closes his eyes and reluctantly nods.

CHAPTER Twenty-Three

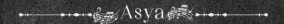 Asya

I COLLECT MY BAG FROM THE BAGGAGE CLAIM CAROUSEL and head toward the arrivals area where family and friends are waiting for the passengers. It takes me less than five seconds to locate Kostya. He's leaning on the pillar further back while several women stand around, gaping at him. When he sees me coming, he walks over to me and takes the bag out of my hand.

"Are we going directly to the fight?" I ask, focusing on his face instead of people milling about.

Most of the men I've noticed at the airport are wearing casual clothes, but there are a few in business attire. I don't freak out when I see men in suits anymore, but I still don't feel comfortable around them. Thank God, Kostya is wearing a hoodie and jeans.

"Yes." He nods and heads toward the exit as I follow. "But I'm still waiting to get the info on the location."

"You don't know where it's held?"

"They switch the places often to avoid police raids. And

since this is the last fight of the season, the exact location will be sent just two hours before the start. I only know it'll be somewhere south of the city."

"Why? Is there something special about it?"

Kostya presses his lips into a thin line and nods toward the parking lot. "I'm parked over here," he says, avoiding eye contact. "We should hurry."

"Kostya? Are you hiding something from me?"

"Of course not, sweetheart." He approaches a black sedan and opens the passenger door for me.

I wait for him to get inside and start the car, then turn to face him. "What's so special about tonight's fight?"

"You haven't watched the last match on the website?"

"You told me not to," I say. "I watched the first ten, but I felt too sick to continue. I assumed the last one was the most violent."

"It was." He nods. "But that's not why I told you to skip it."

"Why then?"

Kostya is silent for a few moments, then takes a deep breath and shakes his head. "I think you should watch it before we arrive, Asya. So you can be prepared."

"Prepared for what?"

When he doesn't reply, I dig out my phone from my backpack and pull up the fight club's website. After I log into the private area, I type in Pasha's name and scroll down to the bottom of the page. Picking the video I skipped before, I click play. It starts like all other recordings, with the aerial view, then zooms in on the fighters. There's an ache in my chest when Pasha's face fills the screen. His left eye is a little swollen, and there's a big bruise on his chin. When the camera zooms out again, I notice that he has a splint from his palm to the middle of his right forearm.

I press my hand over my mouth to stifle a cry. "How was he allowed to fight if he was injured?"

"There are no rules in underground fighting," Kostya says. "As long as he can stand, he can fight."

"What happened?" I choke out.

"He sprained his wrist in the fight before this one."

"Pasha is right-handed. How can he fight with a sprained wrist?"

"He improvises."

I watch as Pasha and his opponent take their spots at the opposite corners. They are more or less matched in size, but the other guy doesn't seem to have any significant injuries. The bell rings and Pasha and the other fighter approach the center of the cage. For a few moments, they stay on the fringe, circling, sizing each other up. Then, Pasha suddenly swings his left hand at his opponent's side. The guy dodges the hit and lunges at Pasha with his fist, aiming for the head. Pasha drops down and swipes his leg just above the floor, catching the guy behind the ankles with his foot. While his opponent is on the floor, he delivers a gut punch with an elbow. Almost as soon as the guy folds, Pasha punches him in the head with his left fist, then kicks him. And again. Blood sprays all over the floor, a few teeth dotting the red stains.

Yelling and cheering erupt from the audience. Pasha rises, grabs the guy by his ankle, and launches him toward the other side of the cage. The fighter lands on his side and stays there. The crowd goes crazy. The camera focuses on Pasha, but I can still see men in nice suits beyond the cage, jumping up, and clapping their hands. The view switches from the fighters to the big screen mounted above the cage. It's an announcement for the next match. The one we're heading to now. Under the words "Big Finale" is a graphic of a red skull and the words "Death Match" are also written in red. The video ends.

I lower the phone to my lap and stare at the road beyond the windshield.

"Are you okay, sweetheart?" Kostya asks.

"No," I say, turning my head to look at him. "What does 'death match' mean?"

He keeps his gaze focused on the strip of dark ribbon ahead and squeezes the steering wheel. "It means the fight only ends when one of the fighters is dead."

I thought I overcame my issue with men in suits.

I was wrong.

The moment we step inside the abandoned factory where the match will take place, I stop dead in my tracks and wrap my hands around my middle. The fighting stage with the chain-link cage is in the center and takes up less than a tenth of the space. Everywhere else, filling the room to near capacity, people are standing in groups, chatting. There are no chairs this time. There must be at least a hundred people, most of whom are men. Some are wearing jeans, like Kostya and me, but most are dressed in swanky clothes. A shiver creeps up my spine, the urge to turn away and run is so strong, I need to gather all my willpower to keep my feet in place.

"Asya?" Kostya asks next to me. "Are you okay?"

I close my eyes for a second. "Yes."

"You don't look okay, sweetheart. Do you want . . . ?" He reaches out his hand and is about to put it on my shoulder, but I quickly step back.

"Please, don't touch me," I mutter. "I . . . I can't handle it at the moment. I'm sorry."

"Do you want to leave?"

I look up to find him watching me with concern. "I'm staying."

"Okay. We'll stay here, in the back. If you want to leave, just say so. Sound good?"

I nod and move my gaze to the fighting cage. It's on the raised platform like in the videos. A man wearing black dress pants and a button-down shirt climbs inside and announces the start of the match, but I can't pay attention to what he's saying because I'm staring in horror at the mountain of a man entering the cage. I press my hands over my mouth to smother a cry.

"Jesus fuck," Kostya curses.

We both gape at Pasha's opponent as he paces inside the cage, flexing his monstrous muscles for the audience. He's taller than any man I have ever seen.

"Don't the fighters need to be evenly matched?" I whisper. The guy is more than a hundred pounds heavier than Pasha.

"Not here."

"What are Pasha's chances?"

"Before the injury? Fifty-fifty."

"And now?" I choke out.

"Not good, Asya," he says and looks down at me. "Let's go wait outside."

I want to say yes so fucking bad. That monster is probably

going to kill Pasha. I heard it in the tone of Kostya's voice, and I don't think I can watch it.

"I'm staying," I whisper at the same moment Pasha steps inside the cage.

The instant my eyes land on him, the tears I've been holding at bay burst out, blurring my vision. I bite the back of my hand, burying my teeth in the skin with all my strength as if physical pain can somehow dispel the feeling of dread. Pasha walks toward the center of the cage and stops, assessing his opponent. I can't help but compare them. My Pasha is a tall guy and heavily muscled, but compared to the beast standing in front of him? Dear God, there is no way Pasha can beat him.

The referee turns away and exits the cage. There is a ring of a bell. Pasha's opponent swings his fist, aiming at the head. Pasha ducks and kicks the guy in the stomach with his left foot. The brute doesn't even move. He swings again, aiming for Pasha's chest this time. Pasha jumps to the right, but not fast enough, and takes the hit to his side. I can't breathe as I watch the opponent close in on him. But before the monster is able to strike, Pasha does a three-sixty spin, and the heel of his foot catches the guy on the neck. Pasha's attack is cut short, however, when a large fist clocks him on the chin.

A scream escapes me as I witness Pasha drop to his knees. He spits out blood and makes a move to stand, but the beast kicks him in the back. The blow is so strong Pasha ends up sprawled facedown on the mat.

"Get up," I whisper into my hand.

My heart is beating out of my chest as I watch Pasha push up, propping himself onto his elbows. He can do it. I know he can do it. He is almost up when his opponent approaches again and kicks him in his kidney. Pasha falls back down, rolling to his side. His face is turned toward the chain-link cage, directly in front of us. The crowd goes crazy. The applause, chants, and hollers are deafening. That damn beast walks around the cage, shouting something at the audience, laughing.

"Finish him!" someone from the crowd yells.

I stare at Pasha, waiting for him to get up, but he just keeps lying there, unmoving. He needs to get up, or the guy is going to kill him. I take off toward the cage.

Several more voices join in the cheering. "Finish him! Finish him!"

People are standing too close together, so I have to squeeze myself between them to get to the front. Bodies are touching me from all sides, making me want to throw up, but I keep pushing myself forward.

"Finish him! Finish him!" the chorus rings all around me.

I finally reach the cage and my eyes find Pasha again. He is still lying on the floor, his face is turned toward me, but I don't think he sees me.

"Pasha!" I yell at the top of my lungs and vault at the cage.

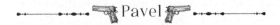

Pavel

"Pasha!" a female scream reaches me.

I blink and focus on the person clinging to the outside of the chain-link cage.

"Get up!" she yells, grabbing the mesh structure with her fingers. "Please!"

I close my eyes. As if it's not enough that I dream about

her every single night, now I'm hallucinating that she's actually here.

"Pasha! Look at me!"

When I open my eyes, she's still there, just a few feet in front of me. If I reach out with my hand, I could touch her fingers where they're gripping at the wire, shaking it.

"Please, baby! Get up!"

My breath catches. "Mishka?"

As I watch, one of the security guys approaches Asya from behind and, wrapping his arm around her middle, pulls her away from the cage. She just grips the metal mesh harder.

"He's coming!" Asya whimpers, looking somewhere behind me. "Get up!"

The guy keeps tugging at her, yelling something. Asya's fingers slip off the links. As the guard carries her away, rage explodes in my chest. He dared to touch her! He put his dirty hands on my girl, and he's wearing a fucking suit!

I roll onto my stomach and rise to face my opponent. He's standing in the middle of the mat, looking at me, blocking my exit. I launch toward him. When my elbow slams into his diaphragm, the air leaves his lungs and he stoops forward. Grabbing his head, I knee him in the face. He stumbles. My leap on his back is swift. Once my arms are coiled around his neck, I squeeze—applying pressure to the back of his head while simultaneously forcing my forearm against his windpipe. The guy starts thrashing around, trying to throw me off. Keeping my choke hold on him, I wrap my legs around his midsection and dig my heels under his ribcage, tightening my grip. He thrashes a few more seconds before he drops to his knees and falls sideways with me still hanging on his back. I keep squeezing, listening to the wheezing sounds coming from his throat. Somehow, I hear them despite the thundering roar of the mob around us. His body goes limp. And I snap his neck. The crowd goes wild. I get up and run toward the cage's exit.

The security guy still has Asya, carrying her toward the back where three other goons are holding Kostya down. A murderous growl leaves my mouth as I sprint toward them. The sea of people splits, letting me pass. The moment I reach the asshole manhandling Asya, I wrap my fingers around his throat and squeeze. His hold on Asya loosens. As soon as she's free, I let go of the man's neck, grab him by the back of his jacket, and heave him to the side.

"Pasha," Asya whispers behind me.

I turn to face her and just stare. I thought I'd never see her again, and having her here, standing before me, is tearing me apart inside.

"What are you doing here?" I bark. It's killing me to be this close to her again.

Her lower lip is trembling as she watches me. The hand she's pressing to her slender neck is shaking. She's trying to keep her gaze on mine, but her eyes wander to the side every other second. I throw a look to the left where she keeps glancing and notice that some of the people from the audience have moved closer and are standing just a few feet away. Most of them are sharply dressed men. Suits and fucking ties!

"Shit, baby," I mumble and take a step forward, wrapping her in my arms and blocking her view of the crowd. "Let's go outside. Okay?"

She tilts her head up and, after a second of hesitation, places her palms on my chest. I close my eyes and inhale deeply. It's hard to have her touching me, to be so close, to know I'll have to watch her walk away again, going back into the arms of that fancy son of a bitch I saw kissing her. But I've already concluded that I'm one selfish bastard, and I'm going to take this opportunity to feel her in my embrace again, even if only for a short while.

I open my eyes and look down at her. "Want to hop on?"

The smile that spreads over her face as she strokes her hands up my chest feels like a knife burrowing itself into my heart. I bend and scoop her up. Asya's arms wrap around my neck like so many times before.

"Release him," I throw over my shoulder at the guys who are still holding Kostya and carry Asya outside.

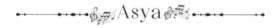

Asya

I can't get enough of his scent. Yes, there's sweat and blood, too, but underneath all that, there's the smell I associate with happiness. Safety. Love. Home. Pasha. Squeezing my legs and arms around him even tighter, I bury my face in the crook of his neck and inhale. I missed him so damn much.

A car door closes behind me, and Pasha gets in the back seat of Kostya's sedan. Even when he's seated, I refuse to let go of him, and plaster myself tighter to his chest. I move my hand up his nape, but instead his dark blond strands of hair, short bristles tickle the skin of my palm.

"Why did you shave your hair?" I ask next to his ear and brush a kiss on the side of his neck.

"Because someone could have used it to gain leverage during a fight," comes his cold answer.

I unwrap my hands from around Pasha's neck and lean back to look at him. His left hand is at my back, caressing me over the fabric on my T-shirt.

"Why are you here, Asya? Did Kostya make you come?"

"No," I say and cup his face with my palms. "I made Kostya bring me here."

"Why?"

I look at his sad gray eyes and lean forward, pressing my lips to his. His mouth is set in a tight line, and he doesn't respond. "Because I love you," I say against his hard lips.

Pasha's body stiffens under mine. "And what happened to your boyfriend?"

"What boyfriend, baby?"

"There's no need to lie. I know."

I straighten on his lap and stare at him in confusion. "What are you talking about?"

He grinds his teeth. "I came to see you last month. I saw you two kiss in front of your house, mishka."

What the fuck? That's nonsense. Today is the first time I've left the house since I returned to New York. I had no desire to see anyone or go anywhere. Unless . . .

I shake my head and reach for my backpack, taking out my phone. "Is this the 'me' you saw kissing a guy?" I ask and turn the screen toward him.

Pasha looks down at the phone, then takes it from my hand and looks closer at the picture on the screen. "Your hair is shorter here." He looks up at me and takes a lock of my hair between his fingers. "And it was shorter when I saw you."

"The woman you saw was Sienna. My sister." I smile. "We're identical twins. I thought I mentioned it."

Pasha lets go of my hair and grabs me behind my neck. "It wasn't you?"

"Of course it wasn't me. I can't even stomach the idea of touching any man other than you."

His jaw clenches and he brings his forehead to rest against mine.

"You're staying," he bites out. "I know I'm selfish. And I know you deserve better. But I don't really give a fuck, Asya. You are staying. And if anyone tries to take you away from me, I'm going to fucking kill them on the spot."

"If you ever ignore one of my calls again, you won't know what hit you."

Pasha crushes his mouth to mine. His hand comes to the side of my face, brushing my cheek with his calloused fingers. His arm around my back squeezes my waist, almost squishing me. I take his bottom lip between my teeth and bite, then kiss my way along his chin to the side of his neck and inhale his scent again. When I get my fill, I move back to his mouth and let his lips devour mine. It's unlike any other kiss we ever shared. Love. Anger. Hurt. Regret. Longing. Healing. There's a lot, and at the same time, there isn't enough.

"Where to, lovebirds?" Kostya asks from the driver seat.

"Home," Pasha says against my lips.

"Home." I nod.

"I can walk," I say as Pasha carries me into his building. He didn't let me move off his lap during the entire drive.

"I know. But I'm not letting you down," he says as he

approaches the security guy in the lobby to get a spare key. The poor man looks shocked at seeing Pasha in only his fighting shorts, all bloody, feet bare, and with me clinging to him.

I tighten my hold on Pasha and bury my face in his neck, where I stay until we reach his apartment. He carries me directly to the bathroom in his room and lowers me next to the sink.

"I need to take a shower," he says.

"Okay." I nod, slip off my glasses, and proceed to take off my clothes. Pasha removes his shorts and boxer briefs, then starts unwrapping the bandages on his left hand. I step closer and take over, revealing the bloody knuckles underneath.

"Will you keep fighting?" I whisper, brushing the wounded skin. "I don't think I can bear watching you go into that cage again, Pasha."

His hand cups my cheek and tilts my head up. "Then I won't."

I nod and look down at the splint on his right hand. "Can you get that wet?"

"No," he says and unstraps it.

When he removes the splint I notice something new inked on the back of his hand, but I don't have time to look at it in detail because he grabs me around the waist and carries me inside the shower stall.

"Let me see your face." I motion with my hand for him to bend down. Pasha turns on the overhead shower, but instead of bending, he crouches in front of me. Water is raining down on him, small rivulets rolling down his bruised face. He looks terrible.

"Why did you do it?" I ask, brushing the tips of my fingers

224

over the cuts and bruises scattered all over his face. "Why go back to fighting after so many years?"

"I hoped that if I got my head smashed enough times, I would forget about you. It didn't work, mishka."

"Good." I pick up the soap from the shelf and lather my hands.

Pasha doesn't move from his crouching position, just watches me with his head tilted up as I clean the blood and dirt off his face. I try to be as gentle as possible, especially around the bruises on his chin and under his eye. When I'm done with his face, I move on to his short hair.

"Now for the rest," I say.

He stands up and lets me wash his chest and back. There are more bruises there—on his side, stomach, and some on his back—visible even under the ink.

"Jesus, baby." I brush my palm down a wicked-looking purple mark on his stomach.

His arms are in slightly better shape. I wash the left one and move to the right, starting at his biceps, and continuing down to his wrist which is slightly swollen. I carefully lather the skin, then move his hand under the spray and watch as the water washes away the suds, revealing the new tattoo. The image is of a thorn-covered branch, done in black ink, its sharp spines pointing in all directions. Above it is a red bird in flight, its fluffy wings spread wide. It's beautiful and sad at the same time. I place the tip of my finger on the design and trace the shape of the bird.

"It's you," Pasha says and brushes my cheek with the back of his other hand.

"The bird?"

"Yes."

225

I look up from the tattoo and find his eyes watching me. "There's only one bird," I say. "Where are you?"

"I'm not there. Just you."

"Why?"

He dips his head to whisper in my ear. "Because there was nothing left of me after you flew away, mishka."

I squeeze my eyes shut, but the tears still escape. The water from the shower cascades down on us, reminding me of the day when he rushed into the stall fully clothed. I wrap my arms around his neck and press my cheek to his. "You shouldn't have pushed me away."

"I know." His arm tightens around me, crushing me against him. "I wanted something better for you."

I move my hand between our bodies and wrap my fingers around his hard length. The moment I start stroking him, he swells even more. "Come with me," I say, taking his hand. I pull him out of the shower and he follows me to the bedroom. When we reach the bed, I push on his chest lightly until he's lying down.

"It doesn't get better than you, Pasha," I say as I climb onto the bed and straddle his legs. "You're the only man I want."

I take his cock in my hand and tilt it to lick the tip. Pasha's hand shoots up and grabs a handful of my hair.

As I suck—slowly at first, then faster—his grip on my locks remains firm. His breathing gets labored, so I switch to licking. I love it, this feeling of elation that spreads through my chest as I see him coming undone. I never would have thought I would enjoy going down on a man, or how much it would turn me on. But this is my Pasha. And I want to do everything with him. I take him into my mouth again—as far as he can go—and he groans as his warm cum explodes down my throat. I swallow it all.

His chest is rising and falling rapidly when I climb on top of him. His hand is still tangled in my hair, clutching at it as if it's a lifeline.

"I love you," I whisper, "so very much."

He stares at me for a few moments, then presses his lips tightly together. "Are you sure, Asya?"

"I'm sure." I lean and press my lips on his forehead. "Can't you see that for yourself?"

He lets go of my hair, sliding his palm around my neck to cup my face and tilt my head up. I expect to see him smiling, but the expression on his face is serious.

"You're very young, baby," he says as he strokes my cheek with his thumb. "What if you meet someone along the way and decide that this . . . us . . . is not *it* for you? I don't think I could survive watching you walk away again, mishka."

I peer at him for a minute, studying his flattened lips, his crooked nose, and his metallic gray eyes that sometimes say more than his words.

"What is love for you, Pasha?" I ask and brush the back of my fingers down his face.

"The feeling of never being close enough." His other hand comes to the back of my neck, squeezing lightly. "I have the need to somehow absorb you into my chest, so you'll always be with me. Safe from harm. Only mine. Forever."

I open my mouth to say something, but he silences me by slamming his lips to mine.

"I love you to the point of madness, Asya," he whispers against my mouth, "and I really need you to be sure. Please."

I bite his lower lip, then trail kisses down his neck and

lower until I reach his heart. I can feel it beating wildly. With one last kiss just over his heart, I climb off his body and head into the walk-in closet. I open the drawer and slide my fingers over the ties folded neatly inside until I reach the deep burgundy one. It's not exactly red, but it's close enough. I take it out and head back into the bedroom. Pasha's eyes follow me as I walk toward the bed, his gaze focused on the tie I'm holding.

"Mishka?" he straightens until he's sitting on the edge of the bed. "What are you doing?"

"I want to show you what love is for me."

I come to stand between his legs and take his hand, placing it on my chest, just over my heart. "You never asked me why I freaked out because of the ties. One of the first clients used his tie to choke me while fucking me. I thought I was going to die that night," I say and raise the hand holding the tie, then drape the silky fabric around my neck.

"Asya, no." Pasha reaches for the tie, but I take his fingers in mine and lay his palm back on my chest.

"Can you feel my heart beating faster than normal?" I move his hand a little up and to the left. "No. Is my breathing getting erratic? It's not."

With my free hand, I take one side of the tie that's hanging loose over my front, wrap it around my neck twice and tuck the end into Pasha's palm resting on my collarbone.

"Last week, I tried helping Arturo with his tie. I adore my brother, and I know he wouldn't ever do anything to hurt me. My hands were shaking so much that I asked him to do it himself instead." I lift my eyes to meet Pasha's. "Do you see my hands shaking now?"

"No, baby," he says in a strangled voice.

"Every single part of me is in love with you, Pasha. My body. My mind." I wrap his fingers around the end of the tie and, keeping my hand over his, I pull on it. The silky material tightens around my neck. "Even my subconscious knows how great and unconditional that love is. So, yes. I'm sure."

I release his hand and hold his gaze as he unwraps the tie from my neck. He does it slowly, careful not to pull on the fabric, and throws it to the floor.

"I'm getting rid of all of those anyway." He reaches and scoops me into his arms, then throws me onto the bed.

I bounce twice, laughing. Pasha climbs on the bed, but instead of hovering over me, he takes my ankle and raises my leg to his mouth, placing a kiss on my toes. I giggle and try pulling my leg free, but he keeps his hold.

"Stop!" I wail.

"Not gonna happen," he mumbles and moves his lips to the arch of my foot.

When his lips find the supersensitive spot on the inside of my ankle, I put my other foot on his chest and try pushing him away without success. "I'm ticklish. Pasha! No, not there!"

"Everywhere, mishka. I plan on covering your whole body with kisses. Every day."

He trails the line of kisses up my leg to my pussy. I feel his warm breath as he gently kisses it before he buries his face between my legs, sucking at my clit. His hands glide up my legs and under my butt cheeks, lifting my ass. I choke on my breath and grab the headboard above my head, holding on for dear life as he slides his tongue inside me. My thighs and arms are shaking as if I'm burning with a fever, and my mind goes blank, focused solely on the sensation of his tongue on me. Suddenly, his mouth vanishes but, a moment later, I feel his cock entering me. He isn't even fully inside and I'm already close to coming.

Pasha's hand grabs the back of my neck. I open my eyes and find him looming above me, so big and ferocious looking with all that ink. My mountain king. The most beautiful man, inside and out.

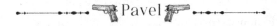 Pavel

I can't take my eyes off Asya's. It's as if they are holding me enslaved. I still find it hard to believe she's mine. Slowly, I pull out only to thrust back into her again, as deep as possible. A small moan leaves her lips while her delicate arms go taut with strain as she grips the headboard above her. The sounds she makes are addictive. I pull out of her again, wrap my arm around her, and turn her around.

"I wish I had the words to explain," I say next to her ear and kiss her earlobe, "how much I love you."

I let my palms glide down her back while I trail slow kisses along her spine, all the way to her ass. Her skin is so soft it feels unreal, and I experience a slight pang of regret as I bury my teeth into her firm butt cheek. Then, I kiss that spot and position myself between her legs, thrusting into her pussy, absorbing her every gasp and moan. I move my left hand lower, between her legs, and tease her clit. Her body is trembling under my touch as my right palm travels up along her spine.

I wish I could touch her everywhere at once. I rock into her with a steady pace for a few strokes, then increase my tempo. Asya lowers her head to the pillow and lifts her ass higher.

"Harder!" she cries out and takes a hold of the headboard again.

I grab her hips and thrust myself deeper. Her walls spasm around my cock, and as I hear her moaning my name when she comes, my restraint snaps. The headboard bangs against the wall while I pound into her like a man possessed.

"Are you mine, mishka?" I bite out between the thrusts. The need to hear her say it is making me insane.

"Always," Asya breathes out.

There are so many things I wished I had in my life, but nothing compares to having her be mine. As long as I have her, I don't need anything else.

"Mine!" I come with a roar, pouring my seed into her.

I tuck Asya closer into my body and pull the blanket over her. It's warm in the room, but I'm always worried she'll get cold. "Does your family know you're here?"

"Yes," she mumbles into my neck.

"And do they know you're not coming back home?" I ask.

I've been dreading this moment. I don't want to fight with her brother, but I will not let him take her away ever again. And if I need to beat the living shit out of him to make him understand, so be it. But what if she can't handle being separated from them?

"I have only one home." She lifts her face to look right into my eyes and smiles. "You. You are my home now."

Something happens inside my chest at that moment. My heart skips a beat, and then I feel something slide into place. The jagged edges finally fitting together.

CHAPTER
Twenty four

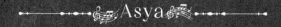

Asya

I'M TAKING THE BOWLS OUT OF THE CUPBOARD WHEN
a kiss lands on the back of my neck.

"I have something for you," Pasha says.

I turn around and stare in confusion at the boxes he's holding in his arms. "New cereal flavors?"

"Yeah." He smiles, but it seems guarded, and places the boxes on the counter. There are five in total.

"Um . . . okay." I snort. "Do you want to pick?"

"No. I want you to choose." He makes sure the boxes are in a perfect line and looks down at me. "Which one?"

I laugh and look at the cereal packages. I rarely have problems with making decisions now, but he still makes sure we practice from time to time. The way Pasha continues to help me is amazing. He even convinced me to meet with the psychiatrist Doc had recommended, and she, too, has been really great. Our sessions are difficult, but I appreciate her care and support.

Reaching out, I grab the box with dried strawberries.

"Does this work for you?" I raise an eyebrow.

"Yes." He leans over and brushes a kiss across my lips. "Now, open it."

Shaking my head, I start opening the box, wondering why he's making such a fuss out of the cereal. I tear the top and stick my hand in to pull out the bag when my fingers touch something hard and velvety. My heart is beating triple-time as I take out a small red box.

"Pasha?" I choke out, staring at the jewelry box. "What is this?"

"I don't know. Let's see" He takes the box from my hand and opens it.

I gape at him as he takes out a gold ring. A radiant-cut yellow diamond shines under the overhead lights. My hand shakes slightly as he lifts it to place a kiss at the tips of my fingers.

"Will you marry me, mishka?"

"Yes," I whisper.

Pasha smiles and slides the ring onto my finger. I sniff and jump into his arms, burying my face in the crook of his neck.

"What would you have done if I picked the wrong box?" I ask.

"You could never pick wrong, baby."

"I could have taken the crunchy cereal."

His palm strokes my back as he laughs. "You hate crunchy cereal."

"Yes, but what if I decided to give it another try?"

He just shrugs.

I lean away and stare at him as realization forms in my brain. "You didn't."

"What?"

I narrow my eyes at him. "Put me down."

"Why?"

"I need to check something."

As my feet touch the ground, I turn toward the counter where the other four cereal boxes are lined up. I take the first one, the one with honey, and open it. A red velvet box sits on top of the cereal bag. When I open it, I find a ring identical to the one on my finger nested on the white silk cushion. I leave the jewelry box on the island and grab the next cereal box. And the next.

The box of crunchy cereal I leave for last. I never would have picked the crunchy one, Pasha knows that very well, but when I open it, the jewelry box is in that one, as well. I put it on the counter next to the other four. He had hidden a ring in each one.

I feel arms wrapping around my waist as Pasha leans on me from behind, but I don't turn. I can't take my eyes off the four extra jewelry boxes holding identical rings.

"Why?" I whisper.

His hold around my middle tightens. "Because I needed you to understand."

"What, Pasha?"

"That as far as I'm concerned, you can't make a wrong decision, baby." A kiss lands at the top of my head. "Even if it's just picking the cereal flavor."

One month later

"What if I freak out?" I ask, my voice sounding strangled.

Sienna looks up from the shoe she's helping me tie up. "You won't freak out, Asya."

"Yes, I know . . ." I lift my hand and bite my nail. "But what if I do? There are like . . . two hundred people out there."

Sienna straightens, pulls my hand away from my mouth, and grabs my shoulders. "You won't freak out. You'll go out there, stand beside the man you love and who's crazy about you, and you'll have the best day of your life."

"I know, but . . ."

"You know, I've been thinking," she says. "When you and Pasha decide to have kids, how about you let me pick out their names? Auntie will make sure they are super special."

I stare at my sister in horror. There's no way I would ever let her pick the names for my children. I'd be risking them being named after chocolate bars or some other candy if I do. Or worse.

Sienna looks up at me and grins. "Relax." She giggles. "I'm just kidding. But admit it, going out there in front of all of those people sounds less terrifying now."

I snort. "It certainly does."

"Everything is going to be fine. Don't worry."

I straighten my dress for the umpteenth time, "Maybe I should have picked a white dress. What if people—"

"It's your wedding day. You can wear whatever the fuck you want, Asya." She looks down at my bright yellow lacy dress and grins. "I love it! You look like you walked out of a fairytale."

"You think Pasha will like it?"

Sienna grabs my face between her palms and leans in closer. "That man is so ridiculously in love with you, you could walk in there wearing a kitchen rag and he would eat you up with his eyes."

I laugh. "I can't believe I'm getting married."

"Me either, sweetie." She sniffs. "Come on. Arturo is waiting. And I'm ruining my makeup."

Sienna squeezes my hand tightly as we leave the room and hurry down the hotel hallway toward the big wooden door at the end, where Arturo is waiting. Leaving me with our brother, Sienna slips inside the wedding hall, pulling the door shut after her. A few moments later, the first tones of a melody reach my ears.

It's not the wedding march.

"Ready?" Arturo asks.

I nod, trying to keep my breathing under control.

The music gets louder as the door before us slowly open. It's "Moonlight Sonata." We step into the hall.

Pasha is standing at the end of the aisle, his eyes glued to mine, following our every step. As Arturo leads me forward, a thought crosses my mind that something is out of order. Considering I'm a bundle of nerves, it's not surprising that the realization hits only when we almost reach our destination.

I blink in confusion. Pasha is dressed in black jeans and a black T-shirt. He knows it doesn't bother me when he wears a suit, so why did he come in jeans? I turn my head to my brother, roving my eyes over his jeans and a Henley shirt until I reach his face.

"Your Russian arranged the dress code for the wedding," he says as he keeps walking.

I take a deep breath and glance at the guests sitting on our left. My heart flutters in my chest. I look over to the right side, as well. It's the same. Every single man is wearing jeans and either a long-sleeved or short-sleeved T-shirt. Even our don, who's sitting in the front row with his wife. I've never in my life seen Salvatore Ajello in a T-shirt. In fact, I don't think anyone has. Except maybe his wife.

I shift my eyes back to Pasha and see him smiling, and I can't keep the tears at bay anymore. So, I let them roll down my cheeks and smile widely as my brother hands me off to my future husband.

Pasha lifts my hand to his mouth and places a kiss on my fingers. "Everything okay, mishka?"

"Yes," I say, "everything is perfect, Pashenka."

We're going through the buffet line when Arturo's phone rings. I turn to the side and pass the serving spoon to the older man standing next to me when I note the tension in Arturo's voice.

"How come they didn't find anything? It's been months."

He listens to the person on the other end of the line for a few moments, then squeezes his temples. "All right."

"What happened?" I ask.

"They still don't have a clue why Rocco's house burned down the way it did, but the report will show a suspected gas leak. No remains were found because everything was scorched to ashes, and the building crumbled in on itself. Based on the security footage before the signal cut out, Rocco, Ravenna, and Alessandro were inside. Without any more evidence, they're closing the investigation and pronouncing the three of them dead." He puts the phone in his pocket and looks over his shoulder. "I need to tell the boss."

I'm staring at Arturo's retreating form when I hear

subdued snickering at my side. I look over at the gray-haired guy next to me. He's piling meat on his plate while a wide smile spreads across his face. What the hell is wrong with him? Three people died, and he finds it funny?

"Jesus fuck, Albert! Are you done?" The big, blond guy standing on the other side nudges him with his elbow. I think his name is Sergei. "Move already, there are other people here who want to eat. And why are you snickering like a damn hyena?"

"No reason." The old guy shakes his head and leaves, quietly singing something. It sounds like . . . "Poker Face" by Lady Gaga.

EPILOGUE

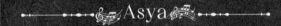

Asya

Five years later

O NE. TWO. THREE. I COUNT IN MY HEAD AS I STARE
at the plastic stick in my hand. One red line appears
in the small display window. Four. Five. Six. Only
one line.

I sit down on the toilet lid and look up at the ceiling. After
I graduated from the music conservatory, I decided to offer
free piano lessons to women who experienced sexual abuse.
I hoped music would be helpful in their healing. Yesterday,
while going through my booked appointments for the next
week, I realized my period is almost a month late. Since I
was done with the school, Pasha and I agreed that I should
stop taking the birth control pills so we could start trying for
a family. I knew that my cycle would get irregular after that,
so missing a period didn't necessarily mean I was pregnant.
It could simply be the side effect.

"Asya?" Pasha's voice comes from the other side of the bathroom door.

"It's negative," I say, trying to make myself sound nonchalant. To hide the disappointment. I was secretly hoping it would be positive. Just the idea of having Pasha's baby made me want to squeal with joy. I was lying snuggled into Pasha's side when I told him I needed to take the pregnancy test. His body went stone-still for a moment, and then he squeezed me against his body so tightly I could barely breathe.

The door opens and Pasha walks inside the bathroom. "It's okay." He brushes my cheek and takes the test from my hand. The expression on his face seems relaxed, but I see it in his eyes—he hoped, as well.

"You're still young. When . . ." He looks down at the plastic stick in his hand and tenses. "Mishka. How many lines should there be?"

"One. It means negative."

"But there are two."

I jump off the toilet and snatch the test out of his grasp. "But there was only one. Give me the box!"

Pasha passes me the box and I quickly read through the instructions until I reach the part where it says you need to wait for at least five minutes. When I read it the first time, I thought it said five seconds.

"It's positive," I choke out and look up at Pasha. He's staring at me intently. "We're going to have a baby."

Slowly, his gaze glides over my chest to my stomach. He takes a deep breath and lowers himself to his knees in front of me. His big hands are shaking as he takes the hem of my top, pushes it up, and kisses just above my navel. Then, he presses his cheek to my midriff and, wrapping his arms around me, starts humming a lullaby.

Pavel

"I already told you, I don't do OB-GYN exams," the doc snaps.

"We have an appointment with a gynecologist tomorrow," I bark and shove him away from the door so Asya and I can get inside his office. "But I need to know that everything is okay. Now."

"You're overreacting."

"I don't give a fuck." With my hands gently gripping Asya under her arms, I lift her onto the gurney. "You can start."

The doc shakes his head and takes a seat, pulling up the ultrasound machine toward him.

My eyes fixate on the scene before me as I watch while he smears some goo on Asya's stomach and moves the device above the waistband of her leggings. He glides the thing from left to right, then rotates it a bit, while keeping an eye on the monitor and hitting some buttons on the tower unit.

"I'd say you're in week six. They both seem perfectly fine," he says, then looks at Asya. "And you seem fine, too."

I blink in confusion. "Both? Both Asya and the baby?"

"No. Both babies."

My head snaps to the side, staring at Asya who's looking at the monitor with a wide smile on her face. "Are you sure?" she whispers.

"Yes," the doc says at the same time as I say, "No!"

They both turn to look at me.

"Do that again." I point my finger at the ultrasound machine while terror seizes me on the inside.

"I'm pretty sure I know how to count!" the doc exclaims and slams the ultrasound printout against my chest, pointing his other finger at it. "One. Two."

I grab the front of his shirt and get in his face. "Again!"

"Pasha?" Asya grips my forearm. "What's going on?"

I release Doc and cup her face between my palms. "It's dangerous, mishka. And you're so tiny. What if something happens?"

Asya presses her finger over my lips. "I'm going to be fine. There are twins in almost every generation of my family, and no one ever had any problems. Don't panic."

"I'm not panicking. I'm not." I throw a look over my shoulder at the doc. "Should she be admitted to a hospital? I'll drive straight there."

"Pasha." Asya pulls at my shirt.

"Can she walk?" I continue. "No, I better carry her there."

"I'm not going to a fucking hospital!" Asya roars into my ear, grabs my chin, and turns my head to face her. "Let's thank the doctor and head home."

"Mishka . . ."

"I wouldn't advise enraging a woman pregnant with twins, Pasha," the doc throws in.

"He won't." Asya leans forward and presses her lips to mine. "Relax. Everything is going to be okay."

The End

Dear reader,

Thanks so much for reading Asya's and Pavel's story! I hope you'll consider leaving a review, letting the other readers know what you thought of Fractured Souls. Even if it's just one short sentence, it makes a huge difference. Reviews help authors find new readers, and help other readers find new books to love!

The next book in the series is **Burned Dreams,** which follows Alessandro (Az) and Ravenna. This is a story of revenge and forbidden love between a bodyguard and a capo's wife. Readers have already asked if there is cheating involved, and the answer is complicated. As Ravenna is married when she starts the relationship with Alessandro, the easy answer would be yes, she cheats on her husband. However, there's more to this situation then it appears at first glance as Ravenna's husband is extremely abusive and violent, and she tries to leave him before Alessandro enters the picture. When Ravenna and Alessandro eventually share their first kiss, there is nothing between her and her husband. So, if the question is if there is cheating between the main characters, the answer would be no.

The publishing date for **Burned Dreams** is July 27th 2023.

NEXT IN THE SERIES

Alessandro & Ravenna

Eight long years, I have been waiting,
Patiently plotting my revenge.
Now, I've found him,
And I'm going to make him pay.

He hired me to guard his wife,
Ensure her safety.
And I'm going to kill
the same woman I vowed to protect.

BURNED
dreams
NEVA ALTAJ

ABOUT THE author

Neva Altaj writes steamy contemporary mafia romance about damaged antiheroes and strong heroines who fall for them. She has a soft spot for crazy jealous, possessive alphas who are willing to burn the world to the ground for their woman. Her stories are full of heat and unexpected turns, and a happily ever after is guaranteed every time.

Neva loves to hear from her readers,
so feel free to reach out (www.neva-altaj.com).

You can access all author links (Facebook, Instagram, TikTok, Reader Group…) by scanning the QR code below.

Made in the USA
Las Vegas, NV
28 December 2024